THE LEGO® 2
MOVIE 2
JUNIOR NOVEL

THE LEGO® MOVIE 2

JUNIOR NOVEL

Adapted by
Kate Howard
Story by Phil Lord & Christopher Miller
Screenplay by Phil Lord & Christopher Miller
and Matthew Fogel
Based on LEGO® Construction Toys

Scholastic Inc.

All rights reserved. Published by Scholastic Inc., *Publishers since 1920.* SCHOLASTIC and associated logos are trademarks and/or registered trademarks of Scholastic Inc.

The publisher does not have any control over and does not assume any responsibility for author or third-party websites or their content.

This book is a work of fiction. Names, characters, places, and incidents are either the product of the author's imagination or are used fictitiously, and any resemblance to actual persons, living or dead, business establishments, events, or locales is entirely coincidental.

ISBN 978-1-338-30759-7

10 9 8 7 6 5 4 3 2 1   19 20 21 22 23

Printed in the U.S.A.   40

First printing 2019

Book design by Jessica Meltzer

CONTENTS

PROLOGUE
AKA
WHAT HAPPENED AFTER TACO TUESDAY

Emmet Brickowski was a lucky guy. He had just banded together with an unlikely group of heroes—Lucy, Batman, Unikitty, the pirate Metalbeard, and spaceman Benny—to fight back for the common good. But then Taco Tuesday happened, and Emmet's town of Bricksburg was never the same again.

That was because on Taco Tuesday, evil aliens from the DUPLO Planet descended and began to wreck the once-beautiful city.

"We're here from the DUPLO Planet," the evil beasts had bellowed. "And we're here to destroy you!"

"You're going to have to get past us!" tough, fearless Lucy cried.

"And me," Batman snarled.

"Oh, it's on," Unikitty hissed in her fiercest voice. The unicorn-cat mash-up was deceptively tough for such an adorable creature.

"YARR!" Metalbeard said.

That's when Emmet had stepped up, ready to fight in his own way. "Wait, guys," he told his friends. "There's no need to fight anymore. I got this."

Lucy shook her head—she'd never really gotten behind Emmet's style of conflict resolution. She always thought he needed to be tougher.

But Emmet disagreed. It was always worth trying kindness first. Sometimes, people could surprise you.

Emmet turned to the DUPLO aliens, softly calling out, "Hello, visitors from another planet! You are just as special as we are." He collected a pile of bricks, quickly master-building them into the shape of a heart. "See? Friends."

One of the aliens crept forward, ready to take it from him. "Ooh," it said.

"Yes," Emmet crooned, moving toward the creature.

Then, seconds later, the DUPLO beast snatched

up the heart, tossed it into its mouth, and gobbled it up. "MORE!" it cried.

Emmet gasped. In this case, he'd been wrong. But it had still been worth a shot. He and his friends slowly backed away as the DUPLO alien's head opened and beamed the bricks up to their mother ship. "More," the beast chanted. Soon, the other DUPLO aliens got in on the chant. "More, more, more, more . . ."

More spaceships had surrounded the group by then, ready to take over the entire city. Emmet and his friends were vastly outnumbered.

In response, Lucy screamed out, "Attack!" Then, with the nimble hands of a skilled Master Builder, she assembled a giant mallet to attack the DUPLO invader. But even with the heroes' master-building skills, they were no match for the massive DUPLO army.

Everyone in Bricksburg had screamed out in horror as their enemies pushed forward, charging through the city like angry beasts.

"Fire the laser cannons!" Metalbeard ordered. He and Benny quickly assembled a cannon and shot lasers at the approaching army. But the

DUPLO aliens opened their mouths and swallowed up the ammunition.

"I eat lasers!" one of them cried, munching away happily.

"That's impossible," Metalbeard said, stumped.

Batman swung between buildings, shooting cannons from above. But the cannonballs simply bounced off their targets like rubber balls.

"You missed me," taunted one of the DUPLO aliens.

"No, I did not!" Batman snapped back.

The DUPLO creatures continued to rage through the city. They pulled apart buildings and happily stomped on anything in their path. *"La la la!"* they crooned, delighted by their destruction.

"Go away!" Lucy hollered. "Leave us alone!"

That's when Bricksburg's onetime leader, Lord Business, got involved. "Guys!" he cried out to the citizens in a reassuring tone. "Everyone get along!" But as soon as he got caught up in the chaos, he gulped. "Well," he said, swinging a big golf bag over his shoulder, "I did what I could. I'm going golfing."

"Wait a minute," Emmet pleaded with him. "You have to stay and help us!"

Lord Business slid into his golf cart and put his foot on the gas. "I'm sorry," he said, with a casual flick of his hand. "I'm sure you guys can sort it out among yourselves!" Then he zoomed off as fast as was possible.

Emmet had watched as their once all-powerful leader set off across the destroyed city, leaving his people alone to fend for themselves. Craning his neck, he gazed up at the looming DUPLO creatures, who far outnumbered the remaining good guys. He was completely unsure of how they could possibly get themselves out of the mess they were in. At the time, he hadn't realized there *was* no way out. There was no way he could have guessed how much could change in one day.

He patted Lucy on the back and said, almost reassuringly, "Don't worry, Lucy. Everything can still be awesome?"

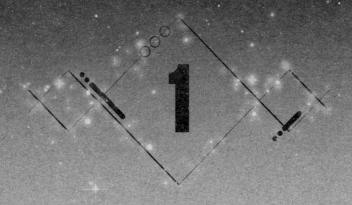

Unfortunately, Emmet was very, very wrong.

Nothing was awesome anymore. The years after Taco Tuesday were marked with battles, relentless suffering, and people living without a shred of hope. Bricksburg was left in ruins. The once-colorful city had turned into a wasteland known as Apocalypseburg.

In a stroke of good fortune, a team of brave heroes—the mighty Justice League—volunteered to chase the aliens back to wherever they came from. Wonder Woman, Superman, and the rest of the Justice League waved to their adoring crowds as they prepared to board their ship. Around them, the DUPLO invaders continued their destruction.

"Hey, where's Batman?" asked Lex Luthor. Superman's nemesis scratched his bald head and searched the crowd for the black-caped hero.

Wonder Woman rolled her eyes. "He's off having his separate adventure," she said. Then she and the rest of the Justice League stepped aboard their ship.

Moments later, the crowd below breathed a sigh of relief—surely, the Justice League would put an end to this destruction, once and for all.

But as they watched the ship climb into the blackened sky, it exploded.

Lucy picked up a piece of debris. "But . . ." she began, shaking her head sadly. "They never even made it past the dreaded Stairgate."

That was the day everyone lost all remaining hope—and the will to rebuild.

The Statue of Liberty sank into a pit of fallen debris. Formerly majestic buildings lost all luster and were marked with blackened evidence of the never-ending war. Peoples' homes were destroyed.

But around the wreckage, a new kind of life emerged. Apocalypseburg was built upon and around the ruins of the Statue of Liberty. Much of the new city existed underground, in former sewers and alleyways. The people scavenged what they could, while defending the little that remained of their former lives.

Anyone who showed weakness was eaten alive in this new dog-eat-dog world. Everyone had been toughened and hardened by years of turmoil and despair.

Everyone, that is, except good ol' Emmet Brickowski.

2

(AS IN, TWO COFFEES)

"Two coffees, please!" Emmet called out to the gruff-looking barista in his favorite local coffee shop in Apocalypseburg. The grimy shop was covered in graffiti and full of battle-scarred warriors and black-clad unsavory characters. In the midst of all the doom, gloom, and danger, Emmet shone like a bright-orange smiling beacon, ordering his coffee. "I'll take one black, and one with just a *touch* of cream and twenty-five sugars."

Emmet balanced the coffees in his hands and skipped out onto the sidewalk. With a friendly wave, he greeted his neighbors as they passed. "Good morning, Apocalypseburg!" he called, a bounce in his step as he hopped along. He stepped into the street, then jumped backward, after nearly getting hit by a giant war rig zooming past. "Ooh! Almost ran me over," Emmet said, chuckling. "Classic."

He stopped to pull out his headphones and turn on his favorite playlist—a collection of upbeat pop tunes, including his very favorite of all time: "Everything Is Awesome." Emmet cruised down the sidewalk, carefree and totally oblivious to the chaos surrounding him. "Good morning!" he shouted as a loud and grumbling motorbike screeched past. "Hello, cyborgs!" he said, waving up at two enormous and scary cyborgs that towered over him.

A moment later, two tough guys toppled out of a window, howling and throwing jabs. They were in the middle of a brawl. They blocked the entire sidewalk. To get around them, Emmet gathered up a heap of loose bricks and quick-built a bridge to climb up and over their fight. He whistled as he worked.

"Hey, Surfer Dave!" Emmet called out, waving to his favorite surfing pal. Surfer Dave was busy chainsawing a pile of surfboards. As soon as he cut each board in half, he tossed the pieces onto a raging fire.

"It's Chainsaw Dave now," Dave grumbled in response.

Emmet shrugged. Whatever made him happy!

"Morning, Scribble Cop!" Emmet said, saluting a cop who was riding in a police vehicle carried by robots.

Still balancing his coffees in his hands, Emmet hopped into a construction lift and pressed the button to go up. He gazed out at the view of Apocalypseburg that stretched out before him. It wasn't pretty, but it was home.

As he rode up to the next level of his favorite city, he spotted his pal Benny, hard at work on Metalbeard's Battle Copter. Emmet quickly built a sign out of spare bricks that said, "YOU'RE AWESOME!"

When he noticed the sign, Benny got so distracted he accidentally blasted his blowtorch right into Metalbeard's chest. "Ahh!" screamed the enormous pirate. "Me organs!"

"Sorry!" Benny yelped, turning the torch in the other direction.

As Emmet hopped off the lift, he bumped into his friend Sherry and her cats. "Good morning, Sherry," Emmet called out cheerfully. He looked at each cat in turn. "Good morning, Scarfield, Deathface, MetalScratch, Razor, Laserbeam, Fingernail, Tox, and Toes." He used his deepest voice to boom, "And Jeff."

The cat Jeff meowed back.

Emmet skipped along, greeting the charming and stinky sewer babies with a friendly, "Morning, sewer babies!"

Farther along, Emmet passed Batman's Citadel. Batman relaxed on a turret while his butler, Alfred, delivered fresh lemonade to the Super Hero. "Hey, Batman!" Emmet called out. "How's protecting the city going?"

"This apocalypse looks pretty good on me," Batman bragged.

"Awesome!" Emmet said, responding with a jolly wave.

Finally, he reached his ultimate destination—the

sunken Statue of Liberty, where his best friend, Lucy, was waiting.

When Emmet came up behind her, he could hear Lucy muttering to herself. "Once," she said quietly, "I was a rebel, fighting for a righteous cause. Now, I only fight to survive. Everything *was* awesome. Now, everything is bleak."

Emmet sidled up beside her, his smile bigger than it had been all morning. He adored Lucy, and being around her made everything extra awesome. "Hey, Lucy," he said, holding out the cup of bitter black coffee. "I brought you a coffee!"

"Coffee!" Lucy hissed, narrowing her eyes. "The bitter liquid that provides the only semblance of pleasure left in these dark times."

"Oh my goodness," Emmet said, pounding his palm on his forehead. He shook his head. "Did I interrupt you brooding just now?"

"Eh," Lucy said with a shrug. "This brooding sesh is not really going anywhere."

"Man, I wish I could brood like you," Emmet said wistfully. He had always admired Lucy—for her courage, her bravery, and, of course, for her toughness. Lucy could brood like no one else he'd ever met in his life; she was a total pro.

"Look," Lucy told him. "All you gotta do is stare off into the distance and then narrate whatever grim thoughts come into your mind."

Emmet nodded, trying to erase the smile from his face. In the darkest voice he could muster up, he said, "What if . . . one day . . . there was . . . no coffee?"

Lucy shook her head. "You need to be more like . . ." She squeezed her lips and eyes into a determined expression, and growled, "War hardens the heart."

Emmet nodded again. Squinting, he tried his best brooding voice again. "War hardens our hearts and—"

Lucy cringed. "Okay," she said, not unkindly. Emmet was soft as a lamb before its first haircut. Soft, sweet, and far too nice to every creature he met. He was *not* tough, and everyone knew you needed to be tough to survive Apocalypseburg. "I'm thinking it's more like . . ." She snarled, "War."

Emmet grinned and chirped, "War!"

Lucy closed her eyes. "Nope. Hang on." She

took a deep breath. Emmet made the word "war" sound like some sort of prize! She tried to demonstrate in her best brooding voice again. "Warrrr."

"War?" Emmet said, giggling a little bit. This was silly! He sounded like a puppy trying to get its owner's attention in the middle of the night. Or Unikitty when she saw a pool of glitter. He did not sound like someone who would *ever* be taken seriously. "I can't do this," he said finally. "I'm too happy to see you."

Lucy sighed. "What's the scariest thing you can think of?" she asked.

Emmet held up one finger. "Oh! Come to think of it, I actually had a nightmare about that last night."

"Nightmares are super broody," Lucy said, encouraging him. "What was it about?"

Emmet stared off into the distance. "All right," he said. "It started with this dolphin in a top hat . . ."

Lucy cringed. Not a nightmare. But maybe it was to Emmet? "Uh huh," she said.

Emmet went on, "And the dolphin says in a weird voice, 'It's 5:15 p.m.' Oh! I forgot to mention, his chest was a clock."

Lucy tried hard to be patient and understanding,

but Emmet just wasn't getting it. He was always just so cheerful and optimistic! "Okay," she said. "I'm thinking darker, broodier . . . less fish."

Emmet stared off into space, clearly lost in the world of his so-called nightmare. "Right. And these scary black holes opened up in the sky like a giant vacuum. They started to suck everybody I've ever cared about out of my life." As he spoke, Emmet grew quieter and more serious. In fact, some might even say it was as if he was *brooding*.

"And a wizard was there," Emmet added, in a sudden burst. "He's shouting, 'It's Armageddon!'" He turned to Lucy. "And you disappeared into the void, never to be seen again."

Lucy considered this for a moment, taking in Emmet's serious expression and smileless face. "Not bad brooding," she said.

"Oh!" Emmet replied, grinning widely. "Thanks!"

After a long moment, Lucy added, "That was definitely just a dream, right? Not some vision of the future?"

"No no no no no," Emmet said. *"This,"* he added, pulling out a pair of binoculars and pointing. "This is my vision of the future."

Lucy looked through the binoculars, training them on the thing Emmet told her to look at, far off in the distance.

"A little lower," Emmet guided her, still pointing. "To the left."

Lucy panned down until the binoculars trained on a small brick house in the middle of the wasteland. "Ta-da!" Emmet said, once he knew she'd seen it.

"A house?" Lucy asked, pulling the binoculars away from her face. She looked at Emmet questioningly.

"Come on!" Emmet said, tugging her arm. "Let me give you the tour!"

3

The two special best friends set off toward Emmet's brand-new house, built out of bright, cheerful bricks. It was a cute, colorful home shining like a beacon at the beginning of a cul-de-sac in the dismal wasteland. It was the picture of perfection amid total destruction.

Emmet led Lucy inside, eager to show his very best friend his amazing new home. "This is the living room," he said, gesturing wildly at his cozy sitting area, "where you can *live it up*!"

He traipsed along from room to room, giving her the grand tour. "TV room ... dining room ... Planty's room," he said. Then, whispering, he added, "The kitty cat room." Next, "Meditation room for me, brooding room for you." With a flourish, he led her into the best room of all. "And of course, the kitchen—complete with a breakfast nook, lunchtime nook, and a fireman pole!"

Emmet grabbed Lucy's hand and together they slid down the fireman pole to the lower level.

The pole, Emmet explained, led to the water-slide and the trampoline room. Then they could monkey bar all the way up to the TOASTER room, where they could enjoy toast or waffles anytime!

Lucy stared in wonder as toast and waffles popped up from the walls and floors all around them.

Finally, he led her outside. "And out back," he said, "a double-decker porch swing, so we can always hang together." He held up a pillow that read, "E&L 4-EVA." Then he waggled his eyebrows at Lucy and said, "What do you think?"

"Uh," Lucy said, briefly speechless. "Wow. Um, it's sweet."

"I just thought we could rebuild the future," Emmet said wistfully. "Make everything *awesome* again."

Lucy heaved a sigh. "Emmet," she said, a warn-ing note in her voice. "You've gotta stop pretending everything is awesome. It isn't. Every morning you walk through town singing that terrible, annoying, manufactured pop song . . ."

Emmet nodded. Yes, he did love "Everything Is Awesome." He couldn't help it! It was a great song, and it made him feel hopeful about the future. But Lucy absolutely hated it. "That song really seems to upset you," he said.

Lucy shrugged. "Lord Business used that music to control us!" she said, recalling an old memory.

"Oh," Emmet said. "Right."

"Babes," Lucy said, trying to get back to the subject at hand. "This house is great. But it's going to attract aliens and get destroyed. You're looking to the past. It's time to look to the future. I never look back."

"That's so true!" Emmet said. He was glad Lucy had brought it up. She never talked about the past, and he knew it was important to look at the past to have any hope of building a brighter future. "You mysteriously never talk about your backstory."

"No, I don't," Lucy agreed. "I don't even like looking in the rearview mirror of a car." Then, with another heavy sigh, she added, "This place is a war-torn heck hole. We have to be tough and battle-ready. Both of us."

Emmet nodded eagerly. "Yeah, no, I get it. And that's why I've cultivated a totally hard-edged side that's super-tough and—" He broke off, pointing into the sky with a huge smile slapped across his face. "Look! Look! A shooting star. Make a wish!"

The star streaked through the sky, but then turned and shifted course toward the ruined city. "Oh no," Lucy said. She pulled out a pair of binoculars, watching through the lenses as the star drew closer.

"What?" Emmet asked casually. "Can't think of anything to wish for? I always just wish for more wishes. Because you can never have enough!"

Lucy shook her head, lowering the binoculars. "Emmet," she said, her body tense.

"What is it?" he asked, squeezing his eyes tight to focus on his wish.

Lucy built a larger pair of binoculars, then lifted them up to her eyes for a closer look. "It's something new," she said, her voice strained. She called out to Unikitty, startling her awake from one of her many daily naps. "Unikitty! Recon mission."

Unikitty strolled outside, yawning hugely. But as soon as she saw the look on Lucy's face, she transformed into Ultrakatty—a much larger, more aggressive version of herself. The sweet, glitter-loving kitty had needed to call on her Ultrakatty powers much more often than usual over the past few years, in order to survive and thrive in the post–Taco Tuesday world.

Lucy hopped onto Ultrakatty's back. Then the fierce feline howled, "Accessing inner rage! AHHHHH!"

"Let's move out," Lucy called. "Hiya!"

Ultrakatty reared up onto her hind legs and dashed off to investigate the strange vessel in the sky. Emmet followed them on the thricycle he'd built.

It didn't take a lot of investigation for the group to figure out that Emmet's "shooting star" was actually an alien spaceship. The huge, round, teal-and-white ball—a Formidaball—sailed over Apocalypseburg's ruined streets, playing cheerful, upbeat music. Lucy peeked up over the edge of a tall wall, spying to try to learn more about the spaceship. "What is it up to?" she whispered.

"I don't know," Emmet said, bopping along with the fun music. "But that beat is pretty fresh." Emmet danced and beatboxed along in synch with the ship's tunes. After a moment, the ship turned and angled its viewfinder on the three friends.

"Uh-oh," Emmet muttered.

The Formidaball launched something at Emmet, Lucy, and Ultrakatty. That something, as it turned out, was a slim heart. The heart landed on the wall directly under them with a big smile, blinking its adorable eyes. "Hello!" it cried out in a sweet voice.

Emmet, Lucy, and Ultrakatty exchanged a look. *Huh*, Emmet thought, growing curious. *That little heart sure is cute!*

But then the heart began to tick and ring. Lucy's eyes went wide. "Run!" she screamed.

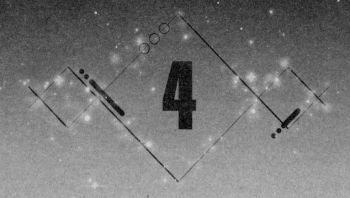

The friends turned and ran just as a tremendous explosion rocked Apocalypseburg. They fled through the streets of the city, trying to escape the strange space vessel. But the ship chased after them, shooting heart-shaped weapons.

Emmet's thricycle was blasted out from under him. Luckily, Lucy spotted the thricycle's wheels spinning uselessly and got an idea. "Super agro turbo engine," she grunted, as she worked to quick-build a getaway car for them. Emmet did what he could to help while also dodging heart explosions.

"Super-safe taillight and blinker," Emmet said, pressing a very important part into place.

"Heat-seeking missiles," Lucy added.

"Windshield wipers!" Emmet said, trying to anticipate all their needs.

Lucy went on, "Spiky blaster cannon."

Emmet jabbed his thinking finger into the air. "Snazzy racing stripes."

As soon as the vehicle was complete, Emmet hopped into the driver's seat. Ultrakatty jumped up top. Lucy slid into the passenger door and hollered, "Go! Get us home as fast as you can."

Emmet floored it. But the alien ship continued its pursuit, chasing the three friends through the streets of Apocalypseburg. It shot heart after heart at them, most of which exploded behind or near the car. But then, two hearts hit the side of a building up ahead. They each trilled the same little alarm clock sound and exploded, causing the building to collapse in a pile of rubble right in front of Emmet and Lucy's getaway car.

"Look out!" Lucy yelled.

Emmet steered their car away from the fallen building. It spun, swerved, and landed inside a skyscraper. Emmet drove through the building, then plowed out the wall on the other side. For a moment, Emmet thought they had lost their pursuers—but then he spotted the alien ship in the rearview mirror. The ship followed every turn Emmet took, no matter how quickly he swerved the wheel.

"It's like it knows our every move," Lucy said, confused.

"Weird, right?" Emmet agreed. He clicked on his turn signal to show he was going right. He knew it was always important to think about safety, even in times like this!

"Emmet!" Lucy shrieked.

"What?" Emmet asked, glancing at her over his shoulder.

"Look out!" Ultrakatty yelled.

A moment later, Emmet plowed their escape car through the wall of the little house he had just finished building, destroying it. Emmet's face fell. He froze, momentarily too stunned to drive.

"Don't look back," Lucy cautioned him, taking the wheel. The house was just a pile of rubble, patches of color splattered across the grim landscape. Lucy drove forward.

Behind them, the Formidaball kept flinging exploding hearts at the trio. Ultrakatty clung to the roof of the car as Lucy swerved to dodge hearts and falling debris. "Ultrakatty," Lucy called out. "Flare!"

Ultrakatty shot the horn out of the top of her head.

Lucy didn't think they could defeat the ship on their own. They needed backup.

5

Batman was exactly the kind of backup that Lucy, Emmet, and Ultrakatty needed.

Batman stood atop the lookout in his Citadel. He saw Ultrakatty's flare rise up into the sky. He knew that signal. It meant HELP!

Whenever help was needed, people always turned to Batman. Batman would describe himself as the greatest Super Hero that had ever lived. He'd also say he was a total stud with arm muscles of steel, a chest and abs that deserved to be featured on billboards, and charm for miles. On top of all that, he was modest, too.

"Alfred," the masked hero said, turning to his butler. It was time to ready the troops!

Alfred turned his megaphone toward the crowd

gathered below. "Send out the battle cars," he commanded.

A horde of warriors began to cheer and whoop. They drove their battle cars out to meet the oncoming attack. Metalbeard was at the front of the crowd in his chopper. "Arrrrgh!" he cried out in his gruff voice as the group charged at the alien ship. "Look on our vehicles and despair!"

But the space vessel easily responded to their attack with a counterattack. It shot a heart out and cleared a path toward Emmet and Lucy's car. Lucy swerved quickly to avoid it.

Metalbeard's Battle Copter fired round after round at the Formidaball, but it served them all back easily—with a tennis racket. One blast landed square on target, sending a Battle Copter blade flying through the air.

The Battle Copter fired harpoons, but the ship simply caught the weapons and tossed them back. The rig's crew members screamed and ran for safety. "Heave-ho!" hollered the warriors inside the rig. "Heave-HO!"

Next, Metalbeard fired sharks at the ship. But the Formidaball turned each shark into a harmless dolphin. Then it fired more of its hearts back at the Battle Copter. One heart knocked Metalbeard's head right off his body and sent it flying. "Yarrrr!" the pirate screamed as his head sailed through the air.

Luckily, Emmet drove past just in time to catch Metalbeard's body parts and pull his pal to safety. "Gotcha!" Emmet said, relieved.

"Ahoy!" Metalbeard called out in response.

It soon became obvious that the citizens of Apocalypseburg could never match the fighting power of the strange space vessel. So everyone ran toward Batman's Citadel—the only place they could think to hide from the attack. Townspeople banged on the door. They called out, "The password is 'password'!"

Alfred hustled toward the door. As soon as he opened it, people flooded inside! But there were some friends who hadn't yet made it to safety— Emmet, Lucy, and Ultrakatty (now Angry Kitty) were still out in the wasteland, racing toward Batman's safehouse and away from the alien ship.

They were so close now that they could see the doors of the Citadel beginning to close. "Come on!" Lucy said as she focused on their target. "The gate's closing."

Lucy quick-built Angry Kitty into the car's motor—they needed her fury for extra speed. "I need thoughts," Angry Kitty said, closing her eyes. To really rev up her motor, she had to muster up as much fury as she could. "Angry thoughts!"

"Angry thoughts," Lucy muttered. "Angry thoughts . . . um, uh—how about people who don't cover their mouths when they cough?"

"IT'S UNSANITARY!" Angry Kitty screeched. The anger she felt over the idea of uncovered coughs powered up her internal motor. She became Ultrakatty. "RAWR!"

Their getaway car revved into high gear. Lucy steered toward the Citadel. "Guys," Lucy told her two friends. "We are going to slide through this very slowly closing door." Behind them, the alien ship was gaining on them, lobbing star missile after star missile. The little critters each cheered as they hit a target. "Whee!" one cried out.

"Hello!" another hollered.

"Hooray!" giggled a third.

If only they could get through the gates, Emmet

thought, *we would be safe*. For now, at least. Emmet and his friends hopped out of their get-away car as soon as they neared the door. They all ran as fast as they could, then made a desperate leap toward the closing doors. They managed to slip through just as the doors were about to slam closed, locking out the outside world. They were in!

But then, one of the ship's star missiles got lodged in the doors right behind them, propping it open just the tiniest crack. The star wriggled and wiggled, trying to get free—but it was stuck.

Up in his tower at the top of the Citadel, Batman launched another attack. He hoped to blast the ship into oblivion now that everyone was safe inside. "Eat it and weep," he growled, firing.

But his giant missiles bounced off the ship like rain pinging off a metal shield. The Formidaball opened a full array of defenses, even as Batman carried out a more extensive attack. "Eat more and weep more!" Batman said, gritting his teeth.

But again, his missiles just bounced off. The alien ship was proving impossible to penetrate! "Keep eating and weeping," Batman snarled, growing angrier and more frustrated with each round of missiles he fired.

Finally, he shot one of the crown spikes off the Statue of Liberty. The spike sliced through the Formidaball's defenses, cutting it in half. *Finally!* The alien vessel exploded and plummeted to the ground.

Batman puffed out his chest. He turned, soaking in the admiration as he was lowered into his throne. A sign lit up on the wall behind him, and Batman gestured to the words as he read them aloud: "You're welcome."

6

nside Batman's Citadel, everything grew quiet. Outside, they could all see a figure stepping out of the smoke and ash of the ruined ship. The figure was unfamiliar and had obviously come from another world. She was wearing a sparkly helmet, a cape, and armor that made her look both sweet and vicious at the same time. She was not at all what anyone had been expecting to see emerging from the strange vessel.

The only person who wasn't paying close attention to the stranger was Emmet. He was busy studying the little star that was still lodged in the door of the Citadel. The poor, adorable little thing was whimpering, and it looked so sad! "Oh, the pain," the star said feebly, pleading with Emmet to release it from its trap. "It's getting so cold here." Emmet felt awful for the little thing! He hated seeing anyone in pain.

But before he could do anything to help the little star, the stranger stepped up to the Citadel's gate. "I'm General Mayhem," she called out. To friends, she was known as *Sweet* Mayhem. "Intergalactic naval commander of the Systar System. Open the gate."

"No way," Lucy scoffed. She shook her head, rolling her eyes at the general. "That gate is never ever ever—"

That's when she noticed what Emmet was doing. He had crept over to the door and was nearing the lever that would open the gates. He felt compelled to free the little star, to let it loose, to end its suffering.

"Emmet!" Lucy screamed, reaching out to stop him from touching the lever. "WHAT ARE YOU DOING?"

Emmet quickly pushed and then pulled the lever. The doors rumbled open and shut just the tiniest fraction of an inch—only enough to free the star and let it head off on its merry way. "Hooray!" the star cheered.

"See?" Emmet said, turning to Lucy with a proud look on his face. He'd done his good deed for the day. "That wasn't so bad. Nothing got in."

Then he glanced over his shoulder and saw that something—some*one*—actually got in. Somehow the space general had slipped in through the crack of the open door and now she was standing right here in Batman's Citadel!

"Gah!" Emmet yelped. "Something got in!"

"Bring me your fiercest leader," Sweet Mayhem commanded, standing in front of the crowd.

"Yeah, that's me," Batman bragged. He pushed through all the people gathered in the hall, making his way toward Sweet Mayhem. "This guy. Coming through." The crowds parted, giving him space. "*I'm* the leader. Obvs."

"You?!" Lucy snorted, stepping forward. "I don't think so."

"How many movies have they made about you?" Batman replied haughtily. "Because there are, like, nine about me. And, like, three others in various stages of development."

Metalbeard came forward then. "Batten yer

hatches," he bellowed angrily. "If *ye* be considered a leader, then why arrrrren't we?"

"Yeah!" Unikitty chimed in. "I'm a princess!"

"I'm *literally* the captain of a pirate ship," Metalbeard growled.

Suddenly, everyone was shouting and yelling over each other, eager to be dubbed the leader of the pack. Sweet Mayhem watched the argument, growing more and more amused by the group.

While everyone was distracted, the space general quietly typed a command into her wristwatch. In the next moment, right outside the Citadel, her destroyed ship began to reassemble itself. Then Sweet Mayhem tapped her foot, waiting for the fighting to subside.

Finally, Emmet stepped forward. "W-w-wait a minute," he said, fumbling for the right words. "When everyone became The Special, didn't we *all* become leaders?"

The Special was a prophesied person who would find a special brick that could stop a superweapon called the Kragle. Before Taco Tuesday, Emmet helped everyone realize that self-belief made someone The Special. Now they were all

The Special! What was Sweet Mayhem getting on about, there being one leader for Apocalypseburg?

"No offense, I sense no leadership qualities from you," Sweet Mayhem said quietly, finally deciding to add her thoughts to the argument. She flicked her chin in Emmet's direction. Inside her helmet, the general's monitors scanned Emmet. She went on, "My readout confirms you to be a less-than-worthy opponent."

"Hey," Lucy snapped. "You watch what you say about Emmet. He saved the universe a few years back."

"*This* guy was a fierce warrior?" Sweet Mayhem said, her voice dripping with disbelief.

"Okay, well," Lucy admitted. "Technically *I* did the warrior stuff, but—"

Sweet Mayhem cut her off. "So *you* fought and master-built and kicked butt, and then the hapless male was the leader?"

Lucy cringed. "Um, well, you know, he was a symbol for . . . that we *all* have ideas, and um—"

Sweet Mayhem tilted her helmeted head. "But *you* did all the work."

Lucy shook her own head. "Emmet is the

sweetest, most optimistic guy you could ever meet. And I know those qualities are not useful anymore, and that Emmet isn't changing with the times, and lacks a killer instinct, and in general just isn't tough enough."

"Not tough enough?" Emmet squeaked. Was that really what Lucy thought of him?

"Yeah," Lucy said, her face set. "But this guy is *The* Special. Well, at least, he *was*."

"Silence!" Sweet Mayhem ordered. Suddenly, her reassembled ship burst through the ceiling. It hovered a few feet off the ground, in the middle of the room. "I don't have room in my ship to take everyone," she said, scanning the assembled crowd. "I can fit maybe five."

"Take?" Lucy said, crossing her arms over her chest.

"Your greatest leaders are cordially invited," Sweet Mayhem announced, "to a Ceremonial Ceremony at 5:15 tonight."

Emmet's eyes widened. 5:15?! That was the time the dolphin alarm clock had gone off in his dream! He closed his eyes, just for a moment, and relived the dream sequence again: The castle exploding, a vortex opening in the sky. It had sucked up bricks and people, including Lucy, Unikitty, and many of Emmet's other pals. In his memory, he could still clearly see Lucy getting sucked upward. She'd stretched an arm out to him and cried, "Emmet! Nooooooo!"

But in the dream, there had been nothing he could do. The power of the vortex was too strong. Lucy had disappeared into the black hole in the sky, and Emmet had watched her go. He'd just watched them all go, totally helpless to save anyone.

Now, reality was looking far too much like that dream. Emmet shook his head, terror locking him into place.

"I got this," Batman said, whizzing past. He fired at Sweet Mayhem, but the shot missed and hit her ship instead.

In response, Sweet Mayhem shot one of her heart weapons at Batman—it floated in front of his face, doling out compliments. "You are so handsome," the little star missile squeaked.

Batman nodded, distracted. There was nothing like a compliment to take away the sting of an attack. "And *you*," he replied sweetly to the star, "are very perceptive."

Just then, an alarm went off and the heart exploded, sending everyone scattering.

Unikitty transformed into Ultrakatty, channeling all her ferocious energy into another attack.

But Sweet Mayhem blasted Ultrakatty with a sticker. The fierce unicorn-cat hit the ground, back in her Unikitty form.

Next, Lucy charged at Sweet Mayhem. The general shot stickers at her, too, but Lucy ducked and they all missed. Instead, they hit Batman in the face! The masked Super Hero was covered in shiny, glittery stickers from head to toe. Lucy raced forward, aiming her blows at the fierce space commander.

Sweet Mayhem went to hit back, and Lucy kicked the sticker gun right out of her arms. It flew up into the air. Lucy lunged for it, but Sweet Mayhem grabbed it first—and blasted Lucy with one of her stickers. This one hit its mark. Lucy was trapped under a giant sticker.

Now, Emmet knew, it was time for him to prove *his* toughness. He quickly master-built some of the rubble into a special Emmet-style mech and zoomed toward Sweet Mayhem. "I'll save you with my *triple*-decker couch, Lucy!" he yowled.

Lucy cringed, fighting to get loose. "You know," she told Emmet, "maybe let us handle it?"

But Emmet wheeled forward, eager to do what he could to help his pals. He knew he could be tough when he needed to be.

Before he could get close, the Formidaball spun, collecting Batman, Lucy, and Unikitty. Metalbeard stepped forward, ready to attack, but instead the creepy vessel smashed his mech body to pieces, then scooped up his head and chest on its next rotation.

Benny raced forward. "Spaceship!" he cried eagerly. The Formidaball scooped him up, too, and locked him in with Sweet Mayhem's other prisoners.

Now it was just Emmet alone. He had to do something, fast. He steered his Triple-Decker Mech toward Sweet Mayhem and called out, "You're pushin' for a cushion!" Then he charged. But his mech was quickly swatted down, collapsing into a pile of loose bricks.

The crowd gasped as Sweet Mayhem's ship

rose up off the ground. It began to lift into the sky. "Lucy!" Emmet screamed, reaching out his arms. He chased after the ship, trying (and failing) to do *something*.

"Emmet!" Lucy called back, reaching her arm out to him.

"Noooooo!" Emmet yelled.

The spaceship sailed up and out of the Citadel, heading for space. Sweet Mayhem lifted one gloved hand and waved to the people below. "So long, Jerkburgers," she said.

Then they were gone.

mmet's head fell to his chest. They were gone. Every one of his best friends, taken by an evil alien space general. What were the odds?

"Emmet," screeched a mermaid who was hanging out nearby. She turned on him with an accusatory look on her face. "What have you done?!"

"You guys, don't think this is all my fault," Emmet replied.

Sherry the Cat Lady shrugged and tilted her head to one side. "Eh, maybe not *entirely* your fault."

Emmet knew there was no sense casting blame. That wasn't going to get his friends back.

It was important to stay positive in times like this! He turned to the gathered Apocalypseburg residents and said, "Lucy and the others are going to be sucked into a black hole—unless we rescue them."

Someone else chimed in, "Who's going to lead the mission?"

Another added, "You're not tough enough to do this. You haven't changed with the times."

"Look," Emmet said patiently. "All we have to do is put together a ragtag crew of unlikely heroes and then—"

The mermaid cut him off. She snorted, "You wouldn't make it past the Stairgate, let alone survive the Systar System."

"That's a suicide mission," offered Harley Quinn.

A wizard added, "Remember what happened to the Justice League?" They all took a moment to remember the day most of the Justice League had disappeared in that midair explosion. "Now with Batman gone, there are no Supers left."

Green Lantern waved at the group. "I'm still here," he said.

Everyone ignored him.

"Aw, come on, everyone!" Emmet tried to rally the townspeople. "We've done this before. We all took on Lord Business and we changed the world. We're all special now, and there's nothing we can't do." He grinned at the gathered crowd, hoping his positive attitude would rub off on everyone else. "We need to go up to that alien planet and show those aliens what we're made of!"

Emmet opened the Citadel's giant doors and marched through them. He hadn't gone far when he turned to look over his shoulder. "Who's coming with me?"

He took a few steps outside the Citadel, then paused to look back again. No one had followed. They were all just staring at him blankly. He waited, staring hopefully at the crowd of neighbors and friends. But still, no one came. Finally the gates swept closed, leaving Emmet alone outside the Citadel. He sighed and walked forward.

No looking back, as Lucy would say. *Only forward.*

He trudged toward his destroyed house. Behind him, the sun was setting on a truly awful day. Outside the wreckage of his house, Emmet reached down and picked up his favorite "E&L 4-EVA" pillow. He could feel the tears coming—but then, something in him snapped.

"I can change," he said with determination.

Then he began to build. He gathered pieces of his scattered home, slowly turning them into something that would be even more useful than a beautiful home. He would build a *flying* house. It would be like a rocket ship, but more comfy!

As soon as he finished building, Emmet strapped Planty into his copilot's seat and took a deep breath. "Hang on to your fronds, Planty. We're going to save Lucy. And . . . all of those other people who were captured."

Someone had to save his friends, and today, that *someone* would be Emmet. With one final look at the ruins of his favorite city, Emmet blasted his house rocket into space. It was time to be a hero!

8

Meanwhile, out in space, Sweet Mayhem guided her ship toward a blue sun. Lucy and the others were tied up with stickers, jammed into the space general's small vessel. They watched out the window as the ship soared toward the far-off Systar System.

"Behold," Sweet Mayhem said, gesturing out the ship's wide front window.

"Whoa," the gang said. They were instantly mesmerized by the garden of colorful planets all lined up in a row.

"No 'whoas'!" Lucy chided. "Don't give her the satisfaction of whoa-ing this."

"Oooooh," the group of prisoners said instead,

eyes wide as Sweet Mayhem swooped even closer to the majestic star system.

"That's even worse!" Lucy hollered.

"Ahhhhh," the prisoners cooed together, further admiring the view.

"Stop it!" Lucy ordered.

The ship headed straight for the blue sun. It descended through the atmosphere, dipping low on the approach. The sun was covered in endless ocean. Light glinted off clear blue water.

Sweet Mayhem steered her ship straight toward a circular waterfall that descended down through the sun, leading straight through to the other pole. When they reached the other side, the waterfall parted, revealing a gorgeous city.

The passengers all crowded in for a closer look.

"Move over," Batman snarled.

"Yer feet be in me face," Metalbeard growled.

Benny whined, "I can't see!"

"Please be quiet," Sweet Mayhem ordered. "I'm trying to make a majestic landing."

The ship floated into a beautiful castle. It landed softly in the center of the castle, then Sweet Mayhem led the prisoners out of the ship.

She marched them along, still in their shackles in a levitating sphere of glittering energy, bound together by the power of a mysterious orb. They took in their surroundings, immediately noticing dozens of guards stationed all around them.

"We're floating," Unikitty noted.

"I know we're not at home," Benny said, his voice reverent, "but do you guys realize we were just in a *spaceship*?!"

Lucy glared at him. "Shut it, Benny."

When they arrived in the central throne room, Sweet Mayhem switched off the orb's power and all the prisoners fell to the floor.

They stood and shook out their legs, getting their bearings inside the castle. Below their feet, mosaic artwork depicted twelve planets circling a watery sun. On each of the planet circles stood a council representative from each planet in the Systar System:

- **Roller Viking Planet**
- **DUPLO Planet**
- **Friendopolis/Capitol: Harmony Town**
- **Cutopolis**

- **Pantryliopolis**
- **Vampiropolis**
- **Monolitiopolis**
- **Anthropormorphia**
- **Planet of Infinite Reflection**
- **Hawkmynotaurus**
- **Ozzieland**
- **Abstractconceptolis**

Lucy and the other Apocalypseburgers took in each of the representatives, analyzing the situation. Suddenly, a talking ice cream cone named Ice Cream Cone waddled forward and said, "Presenting: Her Majesty, Queen Watevra Wa'nabi, Empress of the Systar System!"

Before Lucy could question Ice Cream Cone, or what any of that meant, a platform majestically rose up from the floor. Atop the platform was a beautiful woman wearing a crown and sitting on a horse.

Everyone waited for the woman to speak. But she remained silent; it was the horse that spoke first.

"Susan, would you get our guests something refreshing to drink?" the horse asked the woman.

Immediately, the woman took the crown off and placed it on the horse's head. Then she jumped off the horse's back and bowed. "Yes, your majesty," she said regally.

Susan scampered off, leaving the horse alone on the platform. Then the horse turned to the group with a sly smile. "Welcome, guests, to the Systar System."

"Uh," Lucy said, turning to the other prisoners. "Help me out, guys. What is this, a talking horse?"

"Sorry about my appearance," the horse said. "I was in a meeting with the animal planet of Anthropomorphia, so I look like a horse." She nodded to another horse that was standing nearby on one of the planet mosaics. That horse nodded back respectfully.

The horse wearing the crown went on, "I am Queen Watevra Wa'nabi. I can change my form to something else if this makes you uncomfortable . . ."

A jolt of music came out of hidden speakers, and the queen morphed into a dolphin with human legs and arms. "Hey, guys!" the dolphin said in a chipper voice.

Batman cringed. "No, go back," he said. "The horse was much more palatable."

Lucy stepped forward. She didn't care *what* form the queen was in; she only wanted answers. "Who are you and what do you want with us?" Lucy demanded to know.

The queen transformed into a new creature. "I'll tell you using the universal language," she told them.

"Is it math?" Benny asked excitedly. He loved math.

The queen transformed again, this time into a crown that encircled the group of prisoners.

"The language that unites all the planets in our system," Queen Watevra Wa'nabi went on, as the music grew louder.

"Oh no," Lucy moaned. "It's a song."

The queen beamed. Lucy had guessed correctly. Queen Watevra Wa'nabi began to sing, transforming into new shapes as she continued her song. In the song, she kept reaffirming the fact that she was only planning a ceremony. She wasn't evil at all!

Lucy looked horrified. "I won't lie," she told the

queen. "It's actually very suspicious that you're leading with this."

The queen wrapped the gang up in her arms, pressed a button, and then . . . the castle blasted off! She held her prisoners tight, taking them on an epic tour of the castle and the planet.

Despite the queen's song, Lucy was not convinced.

"I'm getting super-evil vibes here," she said.

The queen wrapped her arm around Benny and sang sweetly to him alone. Then she led Benny to one of the castle's windows and gestured outside to Benny's own special world, promising him a spaceship-building dominion if he took her side.

Lucy shook her friend's shoulder. "Benny, come on. Do *not* fall for this."

Benny couldn't believe the queen was bad news like Lucy said. After all, she'd promised him everything he could ever want! He told Lucy that the queen wasn't evil.

"Yeah," Lucy grumbled. "I know she keeps saying that, but she's clearly an evil queen." She looked over at Metalbeard, checking to see whether he agreed with her.

Metalbeard thrust out his chin. "Yar, well, *I'm* not buying it."

Queen Watevra Wa'nabi had her own plans for Metalbeard. She gestured out another window of the castle, showing him what could be his own new world, complete with a pirate ship and full crew.

Metalbeard was instantly won over.

"What about me?" Unikitty cried.

"Unikitty!" the queen called out in her beautiful voice. "What's the most glitter you can imagine?"

Unikitty replied, "A lot!"

The queen projected an image of a giant Unikitty spewing a glitter waterfall. "Times that by infinity," she promised Unikitty, who needed to hear no more.

The queen struck a regal final pose after she sang the last verse of her song. She'd won everyone over, including Batman—everyone, that is, except for Lucy.

"Sorry. We're not swayed by your little song-and-dance number," Lucy said after a beat.

"Aw," Benny whined. "I liked the tune."

"Let us go," Lucy pleaded with the queen.

"Of course!" Queen Watevra Wa'nabi assured her. "Right after the totally not-evil little ceremony that happens at 5:15."

Lucy shook her head. No way was she going to be any part of the queen's special ceremony. "Whatever you're planning, we will never help you."

"I'm afraid you *must* help," the queen replied with a gentle shake of her head. Then, in a cheery voice she said, "Hey! The drinks are here!"

Susan stepped forward, offering a tray of beverages to the prisoners.

Lucy swung out an arm, knocking the entire tray to the floor. All the drinks crashed to the ground, splashing sticky liquid everywhere. Using the distraction to her advantage, Lucy broke free of her shackles and grabbed Batman's Batarang. Then she Bataranged up to the guards and took them out, one by one.

Following Lucy's lead, Benny, Unikitty, and Metalbeard also attacked. Unikitty transformed into Ultrakatty, whipping out her fiercest claws to fight for freedom.

Lucy took out another guard, then jammed up the steps and knocked out one of the queen's orbs. Finally, she master-built a spear out of the surrounding area and charged the queen.

Just as Lucy leaped, the queen turned into a zero and Lucy flew right through her! Then the queen, thinking quickly, transformed into a giant mallet and knocked Lucy back with the other prisoners.

"Aw," Angry Kitty moaned, only then realizing that the drink tray was gone. "I was thirsty!"

"Girl," Queen Watevra Wa'nabi said to Lucy, "you seem to have a lot of pent-up issues. You know what would help that?"

In a low voice, Batman chimed in, "Dressing up like the animal you fear the most and taking out your rage on law-breaking strangers?"

"No," the queen said, giving him a look. "You need to relax your brain . . . at the health spa!"

"A spa?" Metalbeard growled. "That sounds wonderful!"

"But the way she said it . . . " Lucy said, shivering. When the queen said the word "spa," she sounded like the embodiment of evil.

"Ooh!" Benny cheered. "Can we go, too?"

"Of course!" the queen replied.

"Guys," Lucy pleaded. "Come *on!*"

"You gotta chill out," Batman told her.

"You do seem stressed," Unikitty agreed.

As Sweet Mayhem dragged the group away, Lucy screamed, "We're prisoners! Of *course* I'm stressed!"

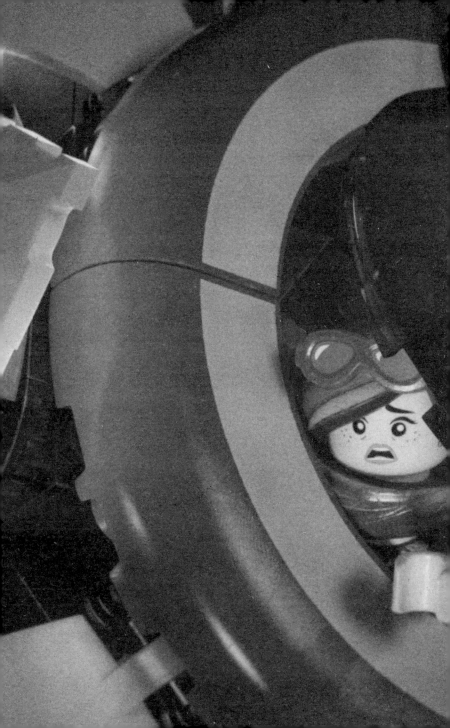

Meanwhile, miles away from Queen Watevra Wa'nabi's health spa, Emmet's house rocket was blasting merrily through space. Inside the flying house, Emmet and Planty were buckled in tight, watching out the windshield as they set their course for the Systar System.

Suddenly, out the window, Emmet spotted a door to a house. But this door wasn't connected to anything, it was just floating in the middle of outer space. Emmet's eyes widened when he realized where he was. "Whoa. It's the portal to dimensions unknown. *The Stairgate*." The door opened then, unleashing a bright light. Emmet steeled himself and said, "I'll just push through the Stairgate. Seems simple enough . . ."

He steered his house rocket through the door and was immediately greeted by a symphony of shapes and colors, stretching and pulling the ship this way and that. A bright light shone down on him, and then suddenly, Emmet was surrounded by asteroids.

An alarm blared. *Wah! Wah! Wah! Wah!*

"Asteroids!" Emmet screeched. Asteroids flew past on all sides, each one nearly knocking his house rocket down! "Torpedoes, deploy!" Emmet said. On cue, waffles blasted out of his house, flinging and flapping uselessly at the asteroids.

"I can do this," Emmet told himself. But then an asteroid blasted one wing of his ship off!

Emmet screamed. "I *can't* do this!" he said, entering ultimate panic mode.

Another asteroid took out his other wing. Emmet closed his eyes as a massive asteroid came barreling directly at his house rocket. He had pretty much accepted his doom.

Emmet braced for impact. This was the end.

And then, in the blink of an eye, a mysterious spaceman appeared. The spaceman flew toward the asteroid, hitting it with a mighty "Chi-*chah*!"

Emmet and his house rocket were saved!

Who's that? Emmet wondered. He wasn't sure what had just happened, but he knew he'd just witnessed some *serious* hero behavior.

The asteroid burst apart before it made contact with Emmet's house rocket. The spaceman zipped past Emmet's front windshield, flying up and over the ship. "Where did he go?" Emmet asked aloud, looking out the windshield.

A moment later, from behind him, Emmet heard a voice. "Hey," the low, rumbling voice said.

"Hey," Emmet said, trying to act cool. But it wasn't every day that a hero spaceman blasted up an asteroid, then mysteriously appeared in your house rocket after essentially saving your life.

The spaceman took the helm of Emmet's ship. Emmet willingly stepped aside to give him the controls. "You mind if I save your life?" the guy asked.

"Not at all," Emmet said, finally breathing a sigh of relief. It was nice to have someone else take the controls for a little while.

"Rad," the guy said. Then he steered Emmet's ship the rest of the way through the asteroid field, dodging and weaving a safe path through the

Stairgate. They sailed through another burst of colors and shapes before finally settling into clear, open space once again. "And *that's*," the guy said, cocking his chin upward, "how you break on through to the other side of the Stairgate."

"Who *are* you?" Emmet asked.

The spaceman popped off his helmet, revealing a dark-haired hero with impressive facial stubble and impossibly good looks. Emmet was blown away by the guy's obvious confidence, toughness, and charm. "Whoa," he breathed.

"The name's Rex. Rex Dangervest." Rex smiled, revealing a row of perfectly straight white teeth. Rex was as supercool as Emmet thought he was: a galaxy-hopping archaeologist, cowboy, and raptor trainer who liked building furniture, busting heads, and having an effortlessly natural smile in photographs.

Just as Emmet was admiring his new comrade, he spotted a huge ship up ahead. "Enemy ship!" Emmet called out. It felt good to rescue Rex right back.

"That's a negative," Rex said, chuckling. "That bad boy is *my* ship. Built her myself out of spare pieces." Then he steered the house rocket right inside his ship, pulling in for a landing in the massive cargo bay. "Let me show you around."

Rex hit the dashboard of Emmet's house rocket and the whole thing collapsed around them.

"Hey!" Emmet wailed. "You broke my ship."

"Listen, kid," Rex reassured him. "You can build anything, but there ain't nothing you can't break."

Emmet laughed awkwardly. "I don't get it."

Rex shook his head and grinned. "How 'bout a tour?" Then Emmet's new friend led him inside the ship's main quarters.

With a wave of his hand, Rex Dangervest announced, "Behold, the *Rexcelsior*!"

"Whoa!" Emmet said again as he stared around at the massive ship interior stretched out before him. It was huge—not to mention crewed by raptors! One raptor stood at a weapon. A few were gathered around a water cooler. Another walked past a huge monitor with a coffee cup clutched in its stubby arm.

Then Rex led Emmet through the *Rexcelsior*'s Skate Park, where raptors were doing tricks and skating bowls. "Whoa," Emmet said, for the millionth time that day.

"Tell me," Rex said, turning to him. "What's a scrapabout like you doing so close to the Stairgate?"

"Aliens from the Systar System took my friends," Emmet explained. "I'm going to get them back."

Rex shook his head. "You don't want to go anywhere near the Systar System. Trust me. It's ruled by an alien queen, and she'll try to manipulate your friends so she can use them in a ceremony to bring forth—"

"Armageddon," Emmet said, cutting him off. He looked out through one of the windows in the *Rexcelsior*, suddenly very serious.

Rex flashed gun-fingers at him. "Bingo. See? You already know. That's why I'm never going back there."

"Wait," Emmet said, quickly putting two and two together. "You've *been* to the Systar System? You can help me!"

"Forget it, kid," Rex said, quickly shaking his head. "What happened to me there was too terrible." He broke off, and then continued in a quieter voice. "But I don't like to talk about my backstory. So don't even ask."

"Oh," Emmet said, nodding. He didn't want to push Rex into anything that made him feel uncomfortable. "Okay."

Rex sighed, then began to speak. "It was five years ago . . ."

Emmet sat back. This was going to be good!

"I was on a galactic mission in that heckish place. I barely escaped, and was tossed in the darkness of space." Rex shuddered at his own memories, which were too terrible to speak aloud. He could remember his ship taking fire, causing him to hit the eject button, then flying out into space. "I landed in the desolate plains of the Dust Planet Undar of the Dryar System. The winds were ferocious. The isolation was intense."

He broke off, shuddering. Emmet waited for him to continue. Clearly, they were already becoming friends! Rex trusted him!

But Rex didn't continue. After a long pause, Emmet said, "And then your friends came to rescue you, right? And everything was okay?"

Rex scoffed. "I waited and waited. No one ever found me."

Emmet felt awful hearing this. "I'm so sorry, Rex," he said.

"Don't be. My time alone was an awakening. I learned how the universe really works." He rubbed one hand across the impressive stubble on his cheeks. Then he set off at a slow walk, Emmet trailing along after him.

"Yeah, I know how you feel," Emmet said.

Rex sauntered over to a pool table. He picked up a cue stick, chalked it up, and then aimed. The ball went right in the pocket he'd been trying to hit. "You couldn't possibly know how it feels," he told Emmet.

"Yeah, I do," Emmet insisted. "Like, you can't ever go back to the person you used to be. And even though it was so much simpler, you have to find your own way. But you just don't know how."

"Hold up a second," Rex said, narrowing his eyes. "You *have* been there."

"Yeah." Emmet shrugged. "And just like you, I thought I was the only one."

"What's your last name, Emmet?"

"Brickowski," Emmet told him.

Rex took a step backward. "No. Way. The visionary double-decker-couch-building hero who took it to Lord Business and had the guts to face the man upstairs? *That* Emmet Brickowski?"

"Yeah," Emmet said.

Rex's smile split his face in two. "Dude! You're a legend, man." Rex was a big fan.

"Wait," Emmet said, confused. "*You* are a fan of *me*?"

"Heck yeah!" Rex said, pounding him on the back. "You're the reason I started wearing vests." He gestured to his outfit, which, Emmet had just realized, did include a vest. "Do you like mine?" Rex asked.

Emmet nodded eagerly. "Yes, I do!"

A raptor squawked something in raptor language. It was calling them vest friends!

Rex hit a lever, and the large platform they were standing on rose up on a track. "As you can see, I made this little vest for my hat as well. Also started wearing chaps, which are essentially leg vests."

The platform stopped moving, and Emmet hopped off onto the ship's bridge. "Whoa," he said. "You've done things with vests I couldn't even imagine." He paused, then asked the thing he'd been thinking about since he'd first stepped foot on the *Rexcelsior.* "Mr. Dangervest, how about you come with me on this adventure to save my friends, and I know we will bond in a deep and meaningful way, and by the end you—you'll never be alone again."

Rex considered Emmet's proposition. Then he slowly shook his head. He called out, "Raptors, re-coordinate!"

The raptor crew punched in numbers on their monitors.

"Really?" Emmet said, shocked.

"Set a course for the Systar System," Rex ordered.

Emmet jumped up and down. This was *great* news. "Rex, I promise, you will not live to regret this!"

"Kid," Rex said, flashing a smile, "I invented the phrase 'no regrets.' I do have one regret—of not trademarking it."

Rex hopped into his captain's chair. "Space cannons!" he cried out.

The raptor crew moved the space cannons into position.

"Hyper-light-speed combustor!"

The combustor fired up.

"Super-rad self-destruct button," Rex added.

The self-destruct button popped up from a seat just as Emmet was about to settle into it. He hopped back up. "Whoa! Isn't there a better place to put that?"

"Raptors," Rex ordered, ignoring Emmet. "Power up! Crank the warp drive up to eleven. Times two!"

The raptors powered up the controls. The *Rexcelsior* fired up and rumbled, whirring to life as it prepared to join in Emmet's epic rescue mission.

"Yeah!" Emmet hollered.

Rex pushed the throttle forward and settled into his seat. As the ship blasted off, he cried out, "To the Systar System!"

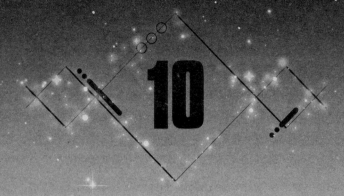

Deep in the Systar System, Lucy and the gang were preparing for their pampering session. Sweet Mayhem led the prisoners toward a uniquely shaped crystal planet that looked very much like a giant disco ball. As she piloted her craft, Mayhem glanced over at Lucy, who was clipped into handcuffs in the passenger's seat.

"What are you hiding?" Mayhem asked.

"What am *I* hiding?" Lucy replied. "What are *you* hiding? You're the one with a face-covering reflective mask!"

Mayhem sighed. "I asked you first," she said.

"Well, I asked you second," replied Lucy.

"Real mature," Mayhem said.

Lucy looked down. She saw one of Sweet Mayhem's heart weapons between them and got an idea.

"Hey, what's that?" Lucy asked, looking up and gesturing at a planet outside the window.

"The Planet of Infinite Reflection," Sweet Mayhem answered. "Where soon you will change your tune."

While Sweet Mayhem carefully steered the ship toward its final destination, Lucy quickly snagged one of the missiles from the heart-cannon cartridge. She slipped it into her jacket pocket without Sweet Mayhem noticing.

"Hello!" the little heart cried out from inside Lucy's pocket.

"What was that?" Sweet Mayhem snapped, glancing over.

"I said"—Lucy made her voice sound like the little missile—"*Hello!*"

"Okay," Sweet Mayhem said strangely. "Well, we've been talking for a while, not sure why you're saying hello now, but fine. Hello to you." Then she shook her helmeted head, focusing on her landing. As soon as they were on the ground, she led a shackled Lucy, Angry Kitty, Metalbeard, Batman, and Benny toward a health spa and mindfulness center.

Inside the center, zen music played quietly. The group passed a gaggle of BrickHeadz, animals, and mini-dolls all getting manicures and pedicures, massages, facials, and other luxurious spa treatments.

After they'd made their way to the front desk, they were greeted by a vampire named Balthazar. He and the other vampires who worked at the spa were all wearing peaceful-looking fluffy robes and had a very quiet aura about them. "Welcome to the Shambhala Health Spa," Balthazar said softly. "Namaste."

Angry Kitty grinned. "Ooh. Sounds spiritual."

"Sounds like a trap," Lucy snapped. "This guy's a vampire—"

Balthazar broke in to say, "Attractive, nonthreatening *teen* vampire."

Lucy rolled her eyes. "We have to focus, stay alert, and not let them . . . " she trailed off, realizing she was the only one still standing beside the front desk. Every one of her friends had already begun their first treatment.

Metalbeard was soaking in a tub, getting a scrub down. "Ahh, yeah," he said happily. "I love getting the barnacles scrubbed off me bilge pump."

Nearby, Unikitty (no longer in Angry Kitty form) was meditating, and Benny was getting sparkly clean. "You should try it, Lucy!" Unikitty said.

Batman was getting a relaxing massage from some animals that were jumping around on his muscled back. "Ahh, yeah," he moaned. "I carry my tension in my delts. Oh, that's good."

"You guys," Lucy said, her voice tight. "Don't fall for—"

Balthazar pressed his cold, white hand over Lucy's mouth. "Shhh," he said soothingly. "Let's be present."

"She needs extra treatment," Sweet Mayhem told the spa staff.

"Yes," Balthazar said in his creepy-calm voice. "First, you'll get a hot stone massage, then some soothing aromatherapy, and finally be cleansed with a glitter scrub and sparkle rinse."

Lucy looked horrified at the thought of every one of those things. Hot *stone* massage? Blech.

After the DUPLO aliens invaded Bricksburg, the once-thriving city became a wasteland called Apocalypseburg.

During this treacherous time, the residents of Apocalypseburg turned to brooding and quarreling.

Unikitty became Ultrakatty.

Batman became even tougher.

But through it all, one Apocalypseburg resident never lost sight of his eternal optimism. That someone was Emmet Brickowski.

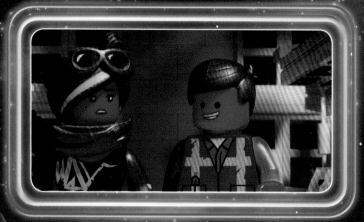

Emmet tried to teach his special best friend, Lucy, to see the glass half-full. But then he spotted something in the sky!

It was a spaceship!

The spaceship launched a heart-shaped device at Apocalypseburg. It exploded! Then the ship's general, Sweet Mayhem, appeared.

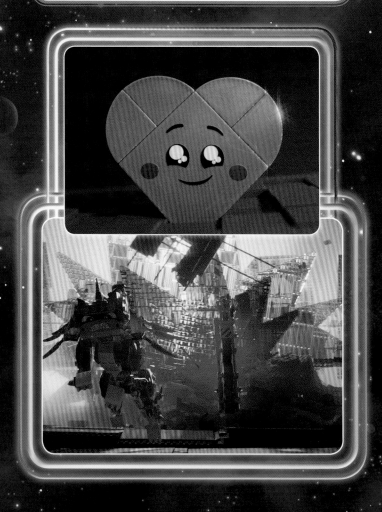

Sweet Mayhem didn't care about Emmet, but she did take all of his best friends and cart them off into space for a special ceremony at 5:15 p.m.

Emmet was all alone. If he wanted his friends back, he'd have to fly into space . . . all by himself! (And with Planty, of course!)

Soothing aromatherapy? Stinky. And *glitter* scrub and *sparkle* rinse? Totally out of character for a warrior like Lucy. But as a prisoner, she didn't have much choice—she'd have to take the torture and survive as best she could.

OOO

Back out in space, the *Rexcelsior* approached a collection of colorful planets lined up with a sun. Emmet looked out through the window, scanning the vast star system laid out before him. "Lucy, where are you?" he asked quietly, knowing he would get no answer.

Rex stood in front of an enormous holographic map of the Systar System. "Finding your friends is gonna be like finding five needles in eleven hay-stacks," he told Emmet.

"Well, that Ceremonial Ceremony that's gonna cause Armageddon is happening at 5:15," Emmet said. "So it has to be before then."

Rex checked the time. "Well, it's already after lunch, so we're gonna need some serious intel. What's your plan?"

"The plan?" Emmet said, his voice wavering. "Um, well, I think—"

Rex cut him off. "We land on the first planet we see, interrogate the inhabitants, find out which planet the ceremony is on, swoop in, and save everyone's butts before the aliens open a portal that sucks everyone you love into an apocalyptic void." He stopped to take a quick breath. "It's a good plan!"

"Yeah," Emmet said, nodding quickly. "That's what I was gonna say."

Rex grinned at him. "Isn't that something? Great minds, I guess. Now, which planet do you want to try?"

Emmet studied the hologram of planets. "Um, what do you think?"

"Emmet Brickowski," Rex said, wiggling one finger in the air. "*You* are The Special. You don't just have what it takes. You *are* what it takes. Now, be decisive." He leaned in closer and whispered, "The raptors are watching us."

Raptors peeked at them from around every corner, waiting for orders.

"But," Emmet began to say, "I really don't know which one!"

Rex sighed. "It doesn't matter if you're right. Just pick any of them and act like you're sure. That's called leadership."

Emmet pointed to a random planet. "Okay— that one!"

"Now you're getting it," Rex said, clapping him on the shoulder. "Woo!"

"Woo?" Emmet asked.

"No," said Rex. "Woooo!"

"Woooo!" Emmet repeated.

"Yeah! Now I feel it!" Rex called.

"I am feeling it and I like it!" Emmet said, his excitement building. "Everyone, suit up!"

Rex began to hand out weapons for their first recon mission. "All right," he said. "We all know this planet is full of aliens. Only the toughest are going to get out of here alive."

As Rex spoke, Emmet mindlessly petted one of the raptors' bellies. "Who's a good boy?" he cooed. "Who's a good boy? Yeah, you are. You're the good boy."

Rex blinked. He liked Emmet, but so far, he was not impressed. Still, this was all he had to work with.

11

The *Rexcelsior* landed in the middle of a lush, rainy jungle. Emmet and Rex stepped out of the vehicle alongside several members of Rex's raptor crew. The raptors headed out first, scanning the area for any immediate danger.

Upon an initial all-clear (or rather, clear *enough*) signal from his raptors, Rex said, "All right, Emmet. Let's go find your friends. But be careful—nothing on this planet is as cute as it seems."

"Yeah," Emmet said, trying on his new tough-guy image. "Cute is, like, for babies."

They set off into the jungle, along with the team of highly armored raptors. As they explored, Emmet took in his surroundings. "Whoa," he said, yet again, admiring the strange new landscape. It was pretty!

Emmet was so busy studying the jungle-like area that he didn't notice when one of the raptors was yanked into the bushes. Its laser cannon clattered to the ground, left behind.

A few steps later, Rex turned and noticed the raptor's absence. "Where's Alpha?" he asked.

Behind them, another raptor was next to be yanked into the bushes, its gear also left behind. Rex scratched his head in alarm.

One by one, each of the raptors ran farther and farther into the lush jungle surrounding them. Rex tried calling out to them, but it was no use. Then, in a whisper, he said, "Nobody move. I'm tracking unusual activity on my unusual activity tracker."

Rex checked his monitor. There were small red dots flashing on the screen, growing rapidly closer to their position. He looked up just as an adorable little creature popped up right in front of him. Rex reached forward and pinned the critter against a tree. "All right, mister," he growled. "Or missus. Tell us everything you know about the ceremony." He shined a flashlight in the creature's face.

"Yeah," Emmet added, trying to sound macho. "Like, where's Lucy? And where are my friends?"

Before the little critter could answer, Rex and Emmet were surrounded by even more adorable-looking, big-eyed alien creatures. These were the Plantimals, who inhabited the jungle on this planet. They began to sing: *"La la la la la!"*

"Oh!" Emmet exclaimed, clapping his hands. "There's a few of them. Hello!" He greeted each of the cute little creatures, one by one. "Hello. Hello. Hello!"

Suddenly, green vines dropped down from above. Rex pushed Emmet back. "Careful, Emmet! Looks like we're outnumbered. We gotta get out of here! Go, go, go!"

Emmet turned and ran just as the adorable little critters bared their teeth and devoured a raptor, leaving only its bones behind.

"Going, going, going!" Emmet yelped. He shuddered. *Yeesh!* He wasn't expecting that.

As Emmet and Rex continued their retreat, the Plantimals devoured another of Rex's raptor crew. Emmet hurriedly picked up all the abandoned raptor gear as he fled. He quick-built a laser cannon truck, then collected Rex and hit the gas.

"Emmet," Rex said, breathing hard. "I told you! Nothing is as cute as it seems!"

The Plantimals tore after the two vest friends through the jungle. "Line them up," Rex ordered Emmet. "Pew, pew, pew, pew!" He blasted laser cannons at the critters, but the Plantimals shot back.

"We're surrounded!" Emmet cried.

"Bust through, Emmet!" Rex said.

Emmet looked at the little Plantimals. They were just so *cute.* How could he possibly blast through them? That wasn't right! They didn't deserve that kind of cruel treatment. But then again . . . they *had* just eaten two of Rex's raptors. And those teeth . . . those teeth were fairly menacing! Emmet took a deep breath, trying to muster up the courage.

"You can do it!" Rex assured him.

Emmet looked at all the Plantimals that had them surrounded. He couldn't do it. "There's too many of them!" he wailed.

"No biggie," Rex said. "Watch this." He faced the adorable pack, steeled himself, and leaped off their laser cannon truck. With a yell, he punched the ground, sending out shock waves that knocked all the creatures back. The horde retreated into the woods, scared away by Rex's blast.

Emmet put on the vehicle's brakes. "Whoa," he said, more impressed by this than anything else Rex had done that day.

Rex turned and walked back to Emmet, acting like his ultra-cool, ultra-tough move was no big deal. Emmet had never seen anyone do *anything* like that! "Not bad back there, kid," Rex said, patting him on the shoulder. "You've got potential. You know, I see a little bit of myself in you."

"Really?" Emmet asked, his eyes wide. "I mean, really cool, *whatever*, I don't care. But . . . how *did* you do that punch thing?"

Rex snickered. "You're a construction worker. I'm a *deconstruction* worker. You see, you gotta break things down to build 'em back up." He lightly punched Emmet's cannon truck and the whole vehicle crumbled to pieces. He went on, "Life's impermanent, always changing. You can't hang on to the past."

"So deep," Emmet breathed. "Hey, you gotta teach me how to do that punching stuff."

Rex nodded. "Start by thinking about an injustice—something that makes you mad. Something like a . . . lamppost?"

"A lamppost?" Emmet repeated, considering the suggestion. Lampposts didn't really bother him, but if Rex got angry about lampposts, maybe he could, too.

But a moment later, Emmet realized Rex had changed subjects entirely. He'd simply been pointing out that they were now standing beside a lamppost that had just flickered to life. As the two guys watched, dozens more lampposts came on all around them.

They had arrived in some sort of town. The darkness around them subsided, revealing a pastel-colored community filled with houses and shops standing in perfect rows. People emerged from their houses doing normal-person stuff: skateboarding, barbecuing, walking their dogs, and playing games. As they passed Emmet and Rex, they greeted the newcomers with a robotic-sounding salutation:

"Hi."

"Hey."

"Hello."

"Hola!"

Emmet was intrigued. "What *is* this place?" he asked.

Rex breathed out a deep sigh. "Emmet, welcome to Heck." Though it was officially known as Harmony Town, Rex had given this horrible place his own *special* name.

While they stood on one of Harmony Town's perfectly clean sidewalks, a kid on a bike wheeled past and handed Emmet a paper that read: "Ceremony Today! Everything will change."

Emmet looked up from the newspaper and noticed a familiar face standing on one of the lawns nearby. "Superman?" he asked, stepping forward. "What are you doing here?"

"Mowing my lawn, of course," Superman replied blandly. "I want everything to be perfect for the Ceremonial Ceremony."

"Where is it?" Emmet pressed. "Where's Lucy? Where are our friends?"

Rex shone his flashlight on Superman, putting on the pressure. "Where's that ceremony?" he growled.

Something grabbed Rex's flashlight, turned it into a bone, and ran off. Rex chased after him, screaming, "Hey! Stop! Stop! Sit!"

As he ran down the street, Rex suddenly noticed something strange about the town. Far off in the distance, right there in the hillside, a slot opened. It was almost as if the environment around them wasn't real. Like they were on a giant set, and people were watching them. Rex squinted, gazing up at the slot. That's when he saw it—a masked face was looking out, watching them.

Rex narrowed his eyes suspiciously, just as the face in the hillside called out to the other guards standing behind it, "Alert the queen!"

11½

nside her castle spaceship, Queen Watevra Wa'nabi was looking out the window when the talking ice cream cone sentry rushed up.

"Your majesty," Ice Cream Cone began. "Intruders have been spotted in Harmony Town."

There was a pause. Then the queen smiled. "Let's give them the old song-and-dance welcome," she said, oh-so-sweetly.

12

Back in Harmony Town (or Heck, depending on which name you'd prefer to call it), Emmet was still pressing Superman for information. "I thought you were going to attack this place!" he said.

"What are you talking about?" Superman laughed. "It's great here. I never want to leave."

"Why—" Emmet began.

"Why don't I have an ice-cold smoothie on a hot day like today?" Superman asked, cutting him off. "My best friend is bringing one to me right now!"

Emmet was surprised to see Lex Luthor strolling toward them with a smoothie on a tray. "Here comes a mango-berry blast!" Lex Luthor said cheerfully.

Superman slurped the smoothie happily.

"Lex Luthor?" Emmet asked while Superman slurped up his smoothie. "Your best *friend* is your sworn *enemy*, Lex Luthor?"

"Is that who I am?" Luthor said, glancing down at his shirt. "Hmm. I thought I was a bald banker or something."

"You don't even know your own name?" Emmet gasped.

Before Emmet could think about how strange this all was, more people arrived. It was Wonder Woman and...Emmet blinked fast. Was that *another* Wonder Woman? Two very different-looking Wonder Women pulled up on a bicycle built for two.

"I can't remember much, either, from before I had that relaxing day at the spa," one of the Wonder Women said.

The other Wonder Woman smiled. "You have to listen to some music!" she advised.

Then a *third* Wonder Woman strolled over. "Listen to the music and let your mind go."

"We should sing the song for you," Lex Luthor told Emmet.

"Great idea, Lexy!" Superman cheered.

Then the Wonder Women counted them off and began to sing. "A one, and a two, and a *la la la la—*"

Emmet covered his ears and turned away. "I want to find my friends! I don't want to listen to a song!"

The big group of Super Heroes continued singing.

○○○

Meanwhile, inside the Shambhala Health Spa, Emmet's friends were nearing the end of their treatments. Lucy had remained tightly wound and on guard through her whole session at the spa. She tried to block out every possible distraction and not let anything get to her.

But suddenly, it was very much impossible to avoid listening to catchy music. The tunes streamed out of speakers all around her treatment room.

Lucy tried covering her ears, but the song slithered in and echoed around inside her brain.

"No!" Lucy screamed, squeezing her eyes shut. "Stop! No!" Finally, she devised a plan. She built a pair of headphones out of the wall of bricks inside her spa room. Then she busted through the wall. On the other side, she found Unikitty listening to the same music inside her chamber. "Unikitty!" she yelled, trying to get her friend's attention.

Unikitty was pink and sparkly clean, and somehow even more adorable than ever. Also, she looked happy . . . *too* happy. The *wrong* kind of happy.

The music carried on.

"Lucy," Unikitty said serenely, bopping her sparkly head to the beat. "Just let go. Sing!"

Lucy cringed. Clearly, this music had some kind of magical power. It was as though it pushed out angry thoughts and replaced them with rainbows, disco balls, and fluffy puppies.

Just then, another one of the treatment room doors opened. Benny emerged, looking equally sparkly and joy-filled. Then Metalbeard stepped out of his chamber, and Lucy was sad to see he also looked downright cheerful. Both guys were singing along.

Another chamber door opened, revealing sparkly Batman, who joined in with the others.

"Guys," Lucy said, snapping her fingers in front of each of her friends' faces. "Snap out of it! What's wrong with you?" But her friends just kept singing, their faces like masks crafted out of clueless, foolish joy.

Unikitty smiled and danced around in floaty circles. Lucy backed away slowly. She felt like the only coherent person in the room as the song droned on.

Metalbeard, Benny, Unikitty, and Batman danced toward her, backing her into a corner. She winced. "Stop it! NO!" She spun and ran toward Balthazar's DJ table. She tried to stop the music, but the song continued. It wouldn't go away!

Lucy spotted a closet. It was marked "PRIVATE: KEEP OUT! CONTRABAND!"

Perfect, she thought, running for the door. She jumped inside and pulled the door closed behind her. A moment later, her friends passed by, not even noticing that she had hidden inside.

From within the closet, Lucy took deep, calming breaths for the first time since she'd arrived at the relaxation spa. "Okay," she said aloud to herself. "So they're not going to help me. Now what do I do?"

She looked around the closet desperately, hoping something might spark an idea. There wasn't exactly a "Stop Sweet Mayhem and the Queen" weapon carefully laid out for her, but there was a ton of props—including a bunch of Justice League stuff!

Lucy poked through the pile of things, unearthing all kinds of familiar treasures. "Wonder Woman's lasso? Ooh, that's Aquaman's trident! Superman's cape?"

She unrolled the cape and a crystal fell out. She studied the cape, noticing that there was a crystal patch sewn onto it . . . and she discovered that there was one crystal missing. Thinking fast, she stuck the loose crystal in the empty slot. Suddenly a hologram of Superman appeared in the closet with her!

Superman was talking fast, obviously in a hurry to record some kind of message. "Whoever gets this message," the hologram said hurriedly, "they're using music to change us! The only way to stop it is to *destroy the queen*! Break the spell; let us go back home. Please!"

The video fizzed out. That was all there was.

Lucy stared at the cape, horrified. What was she going to do?

13

Back in Harmony Town, the very same song that had been playing in the health spa now surrounded Emmet and Rex.

They raced into a house, charging through walls to get away from the annoying and catchy song. Eventually, they dove out a window and fell into a crowd below, where everyone was singing the next verse of the same song.

Rex cried out for his raptors, resisting the song's messages while also trying to save his remaining team.

Emmet called out for them, too, feeling himself getting sucked in by the music. "Help me!"

"Think hard thoughts, Emmet," Rex told him.

"Think hard thoughts! Or the rhythm is gonna get you!"

Rex caught Emmet and pulled him away. Then the two guys ran from the strange Harmony Town crowd, trying to escape the horrible song. *"La la la la!"* Superman sang as he and the other residents chased after them. They pursued Rex and Emmet into an alley, backing them into a corner.

Emmet wailed, "We're trapped! It's a dead end."

Rex checked his tracker. "Okay," he said calmly. "There's a planet right below us." He chose not to tell Emmet that his tracker also said: "ALERT: WEIRD STUFF DOWN BELOW."

"It's our only way out of here," he told Emmet. "I'll hold them back. Emmet, you bust us out."

Emmet shook his head and whined, "I don't know how to do that."

"I know you can do this," Rex told him. "What makes you mad?" Rex began to build a wall around Emmet and himself, trying to stave off the crowds of people.

"They took Lucy," Emmet said sadly. "And the others."

"And how does that make you feel?"

"Not good," Emmet said.

"More honest," Rex urged, still building.

"Super not good," Emmet said, his voice slightly angrier now.

Rex nodded. "You're getting close now, brother. Search deep, find your breaking point. What do you feel?"

Emmet snapped, "I feel very afraid of losing the people I care about forever, and it would be my fault because I wasn't able to change!" He gathered up all the anger he could muster, then unleashed a mighty, rage-filled punch into the ground.

The Harmonytownies all gasped. Emmet had opened a hole to a new world below this one! "Whoa," Emmet said, staring at his fist as though it were some kind of alien appendage.

"Nice job, kid," Rex said, patting him on the back.

"How is there outer space under this sidewalk?" Emmet asked.

"I told you," Rex said, shrugging. "Nothing in this place makes sense!" He jumped through the hole, falling down into the other world. "Also, we can breathe in space here for some reason!"

"Really?" Emmet asked, jumping into the hole after his buddy. If Rex could do it, then he could, too. Emmet was tough now! Brave! He was a whole *new* Emmet.

Emmet screamed as they fell through empty space. Then Rex grabbed Emmet's hand and they fell together—which made it a lot less scary. "Let's do a cool guy handshake," Rex suggested.

"Yeah!" Emmet cheered. "Cool guy handshake!"

They tried a few options and ended up with a high five. It *would* have been awesome . . . if Rex and Emmet weren't also in imminent danger.

○○○

Inside the closet at the health spa, Lucy was at a loss for what to do next. She crept out and made her way through the quiet hallways of the spa. Then she watched from behind a pillar as her friends were guided onto a bus.

"Everyone hop aboard! Buses are leaving right now!" an enthusiastic zebra said.

Lucy muttered to herself as she thought about Superman's message. "Destroy the queen . . . " she repeated and shook her head. "But where *is* she? Where's the queen?"

Suddenly, an announcement came over the PA system. It was the enthusiastic zebra again. "The queen is at the space temple and she wants you all to join her for the ceremony! Namaste!" its voice rang.

Lucy nodded. Well, there was her answer. The queen would be at the space temple. "Okay," she murmured. She considered what her next move should be, but then realized there was only one thing she *could* do. So she dropped down, looked both ways to make sure the coast was clear, and rolled under the bus. She clung to the bottom of the enormous vehicle, knowing this was her only surefire way of finding the queen in order to destroy her.

Moments later, the bus blasted off. Rockets at the back shot it into space. Lucy clung on for dear life as it sailed through the stars. It was difficult, but she knew what she had to do!

14

Rex and Emmet fell for a long time, and they kept doing their handshake the whole way. Finally, they landed smack dab in the middle of some kind of DUPLO construction site, splashing into a pile of loose bricks. Emmet looked around, confused. "Hey, these are Bricksburg bricks," he said, picking up a few loose pieces. "Whoa."

He studied one more closely, but then gently put it down when he noticed a giant, brick-eating DUPLO alien heading straight for them. Emmet and Rex ducked just before the DUPLO monster could gobble them both up. The two guys swam through the heaps of bricks, trying to make their way toward safety. But before they could make any real progress, they were knocked out of the brick pile by another DUPLO monster.

It appeared that they were in some kind of brick-sorting arena. "All right, you guys," called out a DUPLO creature that seemed to be acting as the site's foreman. He was talking to all the other creatures that were hard at work sorting. "The queen says if we don't get these bricks sorted and up to the space temple before the ceremony starts, we'll all be fired. Let's go, go, go! Come on, move it!"

Emmet gasped. "Rex! I think I know what to do!"

"What's your plan?" Rex asked.

"We're gonna have to *hang*, bro."

Rex nodded slowly. "I get it." He leaped onto the shovel arm of an excavator. Emmet jumped up and caught his leg. The force of Emmet's leap spun the shovel around, and the two pals flew through the air, finally landing in one of the sorting carts. This cart was headed toward the temple.

"Well done," Rex said. "The student has become the teaching assistant."

"Thanks," Emmet said, blushing. "I hope this leads to my friends!"

A moment later, the carts were all pulled into a tractor beam, and then Emmet and Rex were sent upward to a gate in the sky.

○○○

Things were not quite as exciting for Lucy on the underside of the bus. For a long time, she clung to the belly of the vehicle as it shot through space. While she rode, she decided to pass the time by working on her brooding. She had a feeling she was going to need every bit of toughness for what she had to do next.

○○○

But the atmosphere *inside* the bus was another matter altogether. Benny, Metalbeard, Unikitty, and Batman spent the whole bus ride smiling, dancing, and having a blast while the enthusiastic zebra drove them to their final destination.

"I am having a great time!" Benny whooped.

"Me too!" Batman cheered. "It's much rad here."

"Yar!" Metalbeard agreed.

The zebra turned up the radio, which had been playing the same song from the spa through the entire drive.

"Yippee!" Unikitty crooned. "Where are we going?"

The enthusiastic zebra glanced back. "We're headed to the big ceremony. But first, Batman, the queen wants to see you."

"Yes!" Batman said, pumping his fist. "I knew I was the leader. In your *face*, Lucy!" Then he looked around. "Wait a minute, where's Lucy's face?"

"Yeah," Benny said. "Where *is* Lucy?"

"Lucy?" Unikitty called.

"Arr, where'd she go?" Metalbeard roared.

"Lucy," the enthusiastic zebra said calmly. "Yes, there is a good answer to that question. And it is . . ." It looked like he was lost for a second, but then he got an idea. "Let's party!" He turned the music up even louder.

"Yay!" Everyone cheered.

Unikitty bounced around. "That was a very satisfying answer to my question!" she said, completely oblivious to the fact that it was *not* actually a very satisfying answer to her question.

Under the bus, Lucy cringed as that horrible, catchy song echoed. Even deep in space, the music *carried*.

"Ugh," Lucy groaned. "No! Stop!" She shook her head, trying to clear the catchy tune out of her brain. "Brood," she coached herself. "Brood. Don't get distracted by—"

She glanced around, searching for something else to focus on. That's when she spotted something moving on the brick cart train up ahead in the distance. She squinted, and then pulled out her binoculars for a closer look. Her eyes went wide.

"Emmet?" Lucy breathed.

Lucy couldn't believe it! Was that really Emmet? *Here?* She had to see him! Even space was jam-packed with traffic, so she flipped off of the bus and began jumping from bus to spaceship to bus, trying to get closer to her friend. But everyone was heading in the same direction—toward a massive space temple in the sky, all for the queen's special ceremony.

Not if I can help it, Lucy thought hopefully.

Emmet and Rex were still inside their carts of Apocalypseburg bricks when Emmet spotted a familiar face coming toward them.

"Lucy?" Emmet gasped. It was definitely his special best friend!

"Emmet!" Lucy cried, hugging him. "How did you—"

"I came to save you!" Emmet told her.

"Who's this guy?" Lucy asked, gesturing to Rex.

"This is Rex Dangervest," Emmet said.

Lucy nodded. She could see that Emmet and Rex were friends, but it seemed like Rex was a bit . . . much. He looked like the kind of guy who would annoy her.

"You look different," Emmet said.

"*You* look different," Lucy replied, taking in Emmet's new look. "Did you draw stubble dots on your face?"

"What? No," Emmet said nervously as he swiped at his cheeks and chin, wiping away the pen marks that he had drawn on to look like Rex.

"The space temple . . ." Emmet said, changing the subject. He stared off into the distance. There, floating in space near the temple, was a fish alarm clock with a digital display that read five o'clock. He pointed. "The clock from my dream! It's all coming true!"

Lucy shot him a look.

He squared his shoulders and continued, "And this is obviously not making me freak out, because I am cool and tough and super not worried." The cart train pulled into the temple. Emmet put on his bravest face. He couldn't wait to show Lucy the *new* Emmet.

"Yep, here we go! Right into the belly of the beast! Super not worried!"

○○○

Inside the temple, the cart rolled on through a tunnel, straight toward a huge smelting oven! If they didn't get out *now*, they would be melted down!

Luckily, Lucy, Emmet, and Rex bailed just in time. They dove out of the cart and rolled, eventually scurrying into a position where they could peek through a tiny hole into a big chamber.

They watched through the hole as puppy people pushed huge wheels that were being used to mix giant cauldrons of nasty-looking molten smelt. The smelt was being heated by billowing flames and then poured into molds on a conveyor track. This track led to giant ovens that would bake the molds into new shapes.

Suddenly, a crew of robed creatures emerged out of a tunnel in the wall. They assembled in some sort of pattern across a catwalk, looking down on the fires burning and puppies working diligently below. One of the figures took off her hood, revealing a cat-headed person. She was obviously the leader.

This lead cat cried out, "Faster! There are only a few minutes left."

One of the other cats turned to her and said, "But we're already working them like dogs."

She furrowed her whiskers. "Then work them like cats."

Lucy was shocked.

"Dogs ... ruled by cats?" she whispered to Emmet and Rex.

Emmet shrugged. He was used to all these surprises by now. "Nothing in this world makes sense," he told her.

The three of them continued to watch the work going on below. On the far side of the ovens, even more puppies were stacking the bricks into a two-story-tall pyramid. "What are they building?" Lucy asked.

"I don't know," Rex replied, "but it can't be good."

"What matters now is how we save our friends, and stop that ceremony so we're not all sucked into a black hole," Emmet said.

Lucy nodded. She wasn't sure about the black hole business, but Emmet was right about one thing—they had to get inside the ceremony. "We gotta destroy that queen," she added.

"Destroy the queen," Rex agreed. "She controls

the minds of everyone here. Defeat her, you'll break the cosmic spell and free your friends."

"Exactly," Lucy said. "So we need a plan."

Rex turned to Emmet. "Sounds like we're gonna need to be in three places at once."

"We split up," Emmet said.

"Great thinking," Rex replied. "I retrieve the *Rexcelsior*, get in position, Lucy locates your friends, and Emmet destroys the queen."

"Uh-huh," Lucy said. "But slight reorder. I'm taking down the queen."

Emmet spun around to face her. "You don't think I can do it?"

"What?" Lucy said innocently. "No, babe. I'm sure you've come a long way. It's just—I need to handle this."

Emmet looked at her, disappointed. "Okay. You go after the queen. I'll find our friends."

"And I'll get my ship," Rex said. "We got no time to lose. Grab a headset and let's break."

Lucy felt bad. She hadn't meant to upstage Emmet, but she knew this was her role. Just as she was about to say more, a shrill voice cried out from below, "Hurry. The icing must be finished before the ceremony begins."

"Icing?" Lucy said, slapping her palm against her forehead. That could mean only one thing! "They're building a cake!" A multilayered cake, perfectly sized for a huge party like the ceremony.

It was time to hustle!

16

Inside the queen's elegant dining room, Batman was enjoying his private audience with the royal. She had called him in so they could discuss an extremely important matter. She had a plan that would unify their two worlds, forever, and Batman was the kind of guy who could help her execute that plan. With his support during the ceremony, there was no way she could fail. Together, they would be stronger than ever.

Batman agreed!

Elsewhere in the palace, a little while later, Lucy was preparing to carry out her part of the plan. She crept around disguised in a robe. When she heard Sweet Mayhem's voice approaching from behind, she ducked into a dark hallway and hid to listen to what the general had to say.

"We must meet the queen in her suite for the final preparations for the ceremony," Sweet Mayhem said to a guard.

Lucy followed behind, careful not to be noticed. Throughout the palace, cheesy music played endlessly through hidden speakers—it was impossible to escape. But Lucy had her orders, and she wasn't about to lose focus now. She spoke softly into a headset. "Okay, target detected. I'm closing in."

In another area of the palace, Emmet and Rex were executing their parts of the plan. "That's a roger, copy niner niner roger copy," Emmet said through the headset. "We're almost to our positions, over copy copy over."

Lucy clicked the headset off. Then she psyched herself up with a quick pep talk. "Just get to the queen's suite without getting tricked," she murmured to herself. "Think hard thoughts. Destroy the queen. Brood. Brood. *Brood.*"

"Did you just say 'brood'?" A guard asked, appearing right in front of her.

Lucy looked up and saw that she'd reached the queen's suite. "No, brewed! Like coffee. Brewed coffee. I have some for the queen."

"I'm sorry, no entry allowed," the guard said. "Who are you?"

"Who, me?" Lucy asked sweetly. Then she switched into battle mode. "I'm your worst nightmare!"

The guard bit his fingernails and whined, "You're me, late to school, and I forgot my homework and my pants are made of pudding?"

"No," Lucy said, baffled. Then she realized there was no sense discussing it further. She just needed to get past this guy. "I don't—"

Lucy paused. This was her moment! She attacked, knocking the guard to the ground. The coast was clear.

She followed Sweet Mayhem and the guards straight into the queen's suite, and stepped inside just in time to overhear the queen say, "Mayhem, is everything in order for the ceremony? I have Batman on board."

Lucy balked. Batman would never help the queen with her special ceremony! Never. Would he?

Sweet Mayhem replied, "I will operate everything here from this home entertainment center of the queen's suite." She walked over to the entertainment area, which was filled with elaborate machinery and complicated electronics.

While Sweet Mayhem was occupied, Lucy rushed the queen. "So much for your ceremony!" she said, charging at her.

But before Lucy could do any damage, Sweet Mayhem shot Lucy with her sticker gun. Lucy dodged, flipped, and kicked Sweet Mayhem into a chocolate fondue fountain.

With a clear shot at the queen, Lucy took her chance. She pulled out the little heart missile she'd stolen earlier from Sweet Mayhem's ship and flung it at Queen Watevra Wa'nabi. The heart zoomed across the room toward the queen, but was caught in midair by Sweet Mayhem.

"Hello!" the heart called out sweetly.

Mayhem shot more stickers and hit Lucy square in the mouth, then bound her arms and legs with even more stickers. After that the general tucked the heart away for later use. She gave Lucy a look that said, "Nice try, fool."

The queen turned to Sweet Mayhem and said, "I told you she'd come to me."

Lucy fell to the floor, straining and struggling to free herself from Sweet Mayhem's sticker binds.

"Take care of her," the queen ordered.

"Mmm-mmmm! Mmm!" Lucy grunted.

Sweet Mayhem brushed herself off. "Are you sure we cannot change her?" she asked the queen, gesturing to Lucy.

"This ceremony needs to be perfect," the queen replied. "I can't have this ... boogawoof wrecking my plans. Get rid of her. Understood?"

Sweet Mayhem nodded. "Yes, my queen."

The queen transformed into an octopus-like creature and headed for the elevator. "The show's about to start," she said. "Mayhem, do the boopity-boop." She gestured to one of the electronic devices that controlled the elevator.

"Boopity bop bop," Mayhem replied. Then she added, "Bring down the house, my queen."

As soon as the queen was gone, Mayhem turned to deal with Lucy. She grabbed two stars and a pole and quick-built a staff with two spinning star saw-blades that cried out *"Wheee!"* as they spun in rapid circles. She then advanced on her prisoner, blades getting closer and closer with every step.

Sweet Mayhem lowered the blades, letting the little stars rip through the stickers that covered Lucy. Then, suddenly, she stepped backward. She couldn't do it. She couldn't follow her queen's orders—not this time.

With a brisk shake of her head, Sweet Mayhem said sadly, "I cannot end you."

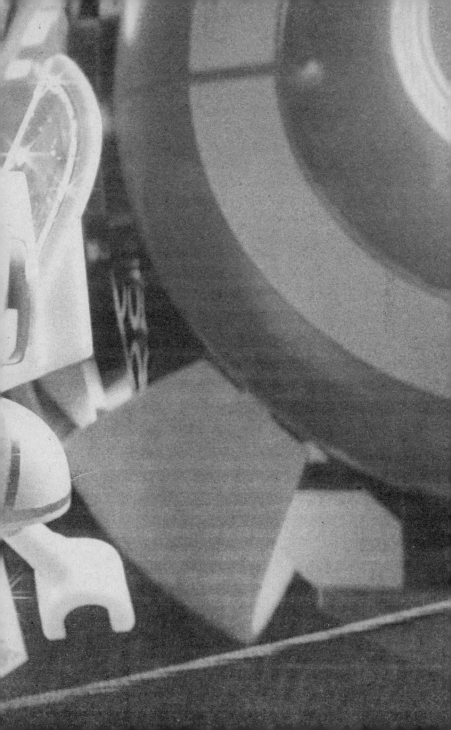

17

nside the space temple, thousands of citizens from the eleven planets of the Systar System had arrived in ships to participate in the big celebration after the queen's special ceremony. The bleachers were filled with creatures hailing from all over the system.

"Citizens of the eleven planets of the Systar System—and assembled Jerksburgian prisoners," cried out Ice Cream Cone. "Let the ceremony commence!"

Below the temple, Rex and Emmet were nearly into position. "Broody Judy," Emmet said into his headset, using their code names. "This is Stubble Trouble. What's your status?" He waited for Lucy's reply. But when none came, he said, "Hello?

Lucy?" He looked helplessly at Rex. "She's not answering."

Rex cringed. "Uh-oh."

"Is that bad?" Emmet asked.

"An 'uh-oh' is never good," Rex said. "I'm worried she might have been captured."

Emmet shook his head. "No, no, no, not Lucy. She's the toughest there is. Lucy?" he called again into his headset. "Lucy? Lucy? Come on, Lucy. Talk to me."

"Emmet," Rex said carefully. "No matter what, you can't let this ceremony happen. If Lucy doesn't go through with it, if she suddenly isn't herself and tries to stop us . . . then she's been imprisoned. It's gonna be up to you to destroy the queen."

Emmet smiled at him. Hearing Rex say that felt good. He *could* do it. He *would* do it.

Above them, right in the middle of the temple, Ice Cream Cone's voice rang out once again. "And now," it said, "I ask you to put your hands together, and apart, and together again in a repeated fashion. Then slide, and twist, and spin, and kick. That's right, go! Keep it going, everyone. Yes! Good!"

Down below, Rex gave Emmet a meaningful

look. "All right. This is where we split. You find your friends, I get my ship, we meet as soon as you finish it. You ready, bud?"

Emmet took a deep breath. He was. Right? "Yes." Then, "No?"

Rex put a headset on Emmet and stared into his eyes. "I believe in you. I've seen who you are. And I know who you can be." He gave Emmet a dark vest, just like the one he was wearing.

Emmet put it on. "Wow, my very own Rex-vest. Thanks for helping me save the world."

"Hey," Rex said with a quick smile. "It was all you." He winked. "Catch you on the flip. Hey-o!" Then he free-fell off the edge of the temple to a one-passenger carrot ship with a bunny rabbit pilot. Rex shoved the bunny aside, then drove the carrot ship off into space.

If Emmet had realized then that this was good-bye, he would have given his new vest friend a hug. But it was better that he didn't know.

As soon as his pal was gone, Emmet focused on the task at hand. The clock read 5:09. It was almost time. Only six minutes away! He peeked over the edge of the temple and spotted his friends in the crowd. None of them seemed like they were going to do *anything* to stop the queen. "Lucy," he said into his headset, knowing he would probably get no answer. "What are you doing?"

Ice Cream Cone continued his speech inside the temple. "Presenting Queen Watevra Wa'nabi . . . and the Man of Bats, Batman!"

The stage filled with smoke. Then the queen and Batman both rose up out of the haze on grand podiums. The queen glanced over at Batman, her willing collaborator. She smiled at him. "Look at us. Two different worlds, so much in common. Both wealthy protectors of our citizens."

"Totally," Batman agreed.

Emmet couldn't believe his pal Batman was *helping* the evil queen. What was going *on*? He spoke quietly into his headset, "Alpha Wolf-Bro Dog, this is Stubble Trouble. Copy?"

Through the headset, Rex replied, "Affirmative. Back in the mother ship. What's the color on the ground?"

Emmet said sadly, "I found my friends. They're all near the top of the temple. You were right—I can barely recognize them."

"Stay alert," Rex warned him. "Do you see the queen anywhere?"

"Affirmative," Emmet said. "And Batman. But I don't see Lucy."

In his headset, Emmet heard his friend say the words he already knew to be true: "This is your shot, kid. You gotta go for it."

Rex went silent. Emmet was alone.

Back in the queen's suite, Sweet Mayhem had just finished explaining to Lucy what was *really* going on—that the queen was having a ceremony that would unite the worlds in order to live in peace and harmony forever.

"Wait," Lucy said, pausing for a long moment. "This whole thing was for peace? Why didn't you just tell us?"

Sweet Mayhem said, "We tried. The queen sang a whole song about how not evil she was."

"That was the *truth*?" Lucy asked. "You guys are terrible communicators!" She took a deep breath. For some reason, she believed Sweet Mayhem now. There was a sincerity in her voice that Lucy could pick up on. "What am I supposed to do now?"

Sweet Mayhem replied, "Help unite the worlds in peace."

Lucy shook her head. "You cannot just take us up here and force us to do your thing and expect peace."

"Well, you can't destroy the queen," Sweet Mayhem said with a shrug. "An act of aggression like that could bring about Armageddon. I mean, who would do something like that?"

Lucy glanced out the window of the queen's suite—she had a perfect view of the space temple below. And in the temple, she could see a single figure running at the queen. She closed her eyes and muttered, "Emmet."

Oh no.

OOO

Inside the space temple, Ice Cream Cone continued announcing the ceremony.

Lucy raced into the temple just as Emmet was running up the stairs toward the queen. "Emmet!" Lucy said, stepping up as if to block him.

Emmet looked at her. "Lucy! Where've you

been? We gotta take down the queen!" He tried to run past her, but Lucy blocked him.

"We can't," she said. "I was wrong about the queen."

Emmet gaped at her, obviously horrified. "Oh no. No no no. Rex was right about you."

"No," Lucy said. "Listen to me. You can't do this."

"I have to do this," Emmet insisted. "You're just stopping me because they talked you into it."

"That's not true!" Lucy spat out.

Just then, Metalbeard, Unikitty, and Benny came up behind Lucy, helping to block Emmet from his mission.

"Ahoy, Emmet," Metalbeard said.

"What happened to you?" Unikitty asked sweetly.

"A betoughening, it seems," Metalbeard said.

The queen glanced from her podium, noticing the ruckus going on below. She turned to Ice Cream Cone and said, "Hurry up, Cone. We're running out of time."

"Guys," Emmet said, trying to shove past them. "Get out of my way!"

His friends all stood there, unmoving. "If ye

want to do harm," Metalbeard told him, "ye will have to get by we first."

"I'm sorry," Emmet said. But he was not sorry. This was his chance to be the hero! "This is for your own good." Emmet raised a fist, mustered up all of his anger about *everything* that had happened, and punched the stairs apart. He was super tough! Bricks and minifigures went flying, clearing a path to reach the queen.

Lucy struggled to reach him before he could do more harm. But another punch from Emmet sent Lucy and more pieces flying. "Emmet!" Lucy screamed. "Stop! This isn't you! What happened to you?"

Emmet turned to her. "I grew up like you wanted me to. Like I should have done a long time ago." Then he spun and raced toward the queen, with Lucy chasing after him.

Just as Emmet reached the top of the stairs—so close to the queen he could almost smell her—Sweet Mayhem piloted the Formidaball into the temple. With Emmet unaware of her presence, Mayhem focused her sights on him and snarled, "I'm taking him out."

Emmet was within striking distance. But just as he reached out for the queen, Lucy grabbed his arm. "Please!" she begged. "Emmet, don't. I like you just the way you were. Sweet, innocent, kind."

Emmet paused. *She did?* He shook his head and said, "The real Lucy would never say that."

He leaped and punched at the base of the queen's podium. The impact sent a shock wave through the entire temple, cracking it open. The whole place began to crumble.

Everyone in the audience started to wail and scream. Lucy was knocked on her side, and began to fall into space. Emmet grabbed for her just as the clock turned to 5:15. "What is happening?" he screamed. Then, "Luuuuuucy!"

Emmet's nightmare was coming true. All his friends were in danger, and the world was falling apart! Was it all his fault?

Balthazar, the vampire from the health spa, suddenly appeared amid the chaos. "Remain calm," he called out. "Practice mindfulness." Then, after a deep, cleansing breath in, he screamed, "I'm freaking out!" Then he was turned into a bat and sucked into the void of open space.

It seemed there was nothing more they could do. Emmet had destroyed the queen's crystal with his blast, but nothing had changed. Things hadn't been reset like he'd thought they would be. Everything was just the same. Suddenly, Emmet felt himself getting sucked up into the rubble. He fell—

Down
Down
Down

And then there was blackness. He'd lost his friends. He'd lost everything. This was the end.

THE END

Turn the page ➡

JUST KIDDING!

20

uckily, Lucy had long ago mastered the art of remaining calm in the face of danger. "It's only over if we give up," she said quietly to herself. "I have to come up with a way to bring us all together. If only there was a universal language that bypassed the brain and went straight to the heart . . ." She suddenly realized the answer: music. Cringing at this realization, she groaned. "Oh no."

But she had no other choice. She had to sing a version of the tune that had brought them all together in the first place. So she began to chant, quietly at first, growing louder with each line.

Unikitty wailed. "Uh, Lucy, is this supposed to cheer us up somehow?"

"I think she lost a jibsail," Metalbeard said.

"Just let her work through it," Benny told them.

Lucy continued to sing. The others joined in, too.

Now Lucy felt confident and ready to make everything right again. "All right, everyone," she said, her voice strong and sure. "We've got to save Emmet!" She quick-built a ship out of the rubble of the temple and then took the controls.

Others had ships, too. Lucy's ship was one of many, all working together to try to save their friend Emmet. In true Emmet style, Lucy's copilot was Sweet Mayhem—the two former enemies were now working together to try to bring harmony back to the world. "Come on, armada," Lucy said hopefully to all the ships following behind her. "We've gotta find Emmet."

Lex Luthor and Superman were flying in another ship together, along with the three Wonder Women. In the back of their ship, Benny sang out commands: *"Hit that switch, turn this knob, hit that lever, do that spaceship thing!"*

Metalbeard and Ice Cream Cone piloted an ice cream pirate spaceship that was a perfect blend of their two worlds. "Heave-ho!" Metalbeard called out. "Weigh anchor and hoist the mizzen! Full sail!" The sails on the spaceship dropped down.

Ice Cream Cone pointed out, "There's no wind in space."

Metalbeard said, "Let me have this."

The cats that ruled over the puppies were now working together to crew another ship in the armada. The dogs tugged at cranks, working the engine in the massive ark of a ship. "Faster!" the lead cat ordered.

"Allow me," Unikitty said, stepping forward. "I speak dog." She barked into a speaker. "Bow wow wow. Bow wow wow. Arf, growl! Yay!"

Moments later, the cat rulers—along with Sherry the Cat Lady and her collection of cats—joined in to help the dogs. When they worked together, the ship began to sail faster.

At the front of the armada, Lucy suddenly spotted an unfamiliar location up ahead of them. "What is that?" she said, pointing. "Maybe Emmet's over there!"

She guided her ship toward the strange planet. Yes! There was Emmet, trapped deep under some rubble, inside a dimension unknown. His body was squeezed inside a space that was far too tight to land a ship. There was no way to reach him.

That's when Lucy came up with her next plan: They would form a chain of friends and pull Emmet to safety. It was risky, yes, but it was their only choice. She couldn't just leave him there. Not after all he'd done for all of them.

"Lucy!" Emmet called out, waving as he spotted her in the ship at the front of the armada.

The chain of friends stretched out, reaching for Emmet. Closer, closer . . .

There!

Emmet grabbed his best friend's hand and clung to her. She pulled him to safety. "I think we should go," Lucy told him. "Time to get back, don't you think?"

"Yeah," Emmet said, a huge smile on his face.

The chain reeled the pair back into Mayhem's ship. As soon as they were safe inside, Emmet and Lucy embraced in a huge hug. "Emmet," Lucy said earnestly. "I'm sorry I tried to change you into something you weren't. Special best friends?"

Emmet grinned. "4-EVA," he said.

Slowly, the armada flew through space, heading toward home. They had done it. By working together for something good, they had united the two worlds in peace and harmony. Everyone celebrated with cheers and hugs all around.

In the days that followed, the rebuilding process began. With everyone pitching in to help, they started to build up a new world ... the kind Emmet had always dreamed was possible.

But most important, everything was finally awesome again!

THE END

(For real this time!)